FOOD CHAIN

VOLUME ONE

T LI

"It was the Law of the Sea, they said. Civilization ends at the waterline. Beyond that, we all enter the food chain, and not always right at the top."

- Hunter S. Thompson

PART I

Mikko Laine completed his first week as the Director of Security at Museokeskus Vapriikki and was on his way home. He spent the day watching monitors that displayed security personnel, who, in turn, monitored visitors examining the exhibits throughout the museum complex. The work reminded him of gazing into a mirror facing another mirror, with the reflections stretching endlessly into infinity.

He walked across the Tammerkoski Bridge toward his apartment. The railings and metal gates along the river rapids were adorned with locks; this was a gesture some couples enjoyed to express their love. Tonight, the locks on the railings glistened with ice, sparkling in the frosty moonlight. In the early morning, as Mikko set off for work, the biting cold wind sliced through his wool jacket, chilling him to the bone. However, this evening the wind had calmed. It was quiet but not entirely silent. There was a steady crunching of the thin layer of snow beneath his boots. The rapids were low at this time of year, and the icy, rushing water gurgled, resisting the urge to freeze and become still. It was colder here. Colder than in the town where he grew up, but he was grateful for the job. It paid well, and as part of the arrangement, they offered an apartment. The spacious residence was situated along the banks of the Tammerkoski River in one of the repurposed old factory mills. From the huge metal windows, he could see the lakes Näsijärvi and Pyhäjärvi. The panorama was grand, but it wasn't the only view that caught his interest.

As Mikko approached his apartment, he thought he heard murmuring behind the door. He dismissed the noises and unlocked it, stepping inside cautiously. A few of his new acquaintances resoundingly shouted, "Surprise!"

His shocked face was met with laughter, smiles, and a rapid explanation from Kaija, the pink-haired girl who worked in the museum's human resources department. Mikko glanced around the room. He knew Sofia, who worked in the museum gift shop, and Nilas from the payroll department. There were two others he didn't know, but he recognized their faces in passing.

"Oh, Mikko. I'm sorry. You looked so stunned. " She giggled and hugged him.

"It's..Uhm, I'm okay, what...what is this?" Mikko stammered and forced a weak smile.

"We do this for new employees after they finish their first week," she explained.

"No, that's *if* they finish their first week without quitting!" Sofia added.

"Kaija is lying; we don't do this for everyone," Nilas grumbled.

"Yes…yes, he's right, only the employees we like." Kaija winked at Mikko, and he blushed.

"Well, thank you…" Mikko murmured shyly, looking at the drinks and snacks that were laid out.

"How did you...who let you in?" he asked.

"Oh, we asked the maintenance guys. They have sets of keys for all the apartments in this wing," Sofia answered.

"Which I find very creepy," Nilas complained.

Mikko sat down and took a piece of Mokkapalat. He was very fond of sweets, and these cakes were delicious. The chocolate and coffee flavors had just the right balance.

"There's nothing creepy about it. They need the keys to fix things. I had an electrical problem last week, and it was all repaired by the time I got home," Sofia said.

" And you don't think they went through your undergarments while they were there?" Nilas taunted.

Kaija and Mikko chuckled. The other two, Onni and Annika, smirked, waiting for her comeback.

Sofia jokes, "They can wear them for all I care, just as long as they return them and preferably laundered!"

Her comment made the group laugh. Mikko was glad he had found a welcoming group of friends. Although he was an introvert by nature, he occasionally enjoyed being in the company of others.

"I just don't like the idea that these maintenance guys can enter my apartment whenever they please," Nilas repeated.

"That's because you walk around naked half the time," Onni remarked.

"Like my neighbor in the opposite building," Mikko said casually and then regretted mentioning it directly afterward.

"You're joking?" Kaija smirked.

"What? And you can see? Clearly?" Sofia questioned.

Onni stood up. He walked straight to the large window, asking,

"This window here? Is she hot?"

Mikko found himself having to provide details for the numerous questions that were asked.

"Yes, it's that window, but it isn't every night… uhm..usually much later in the evening…" Mikko offered reluctantly.

"So it is a nightly occurrence?" Kaija commented.

"Will you sit down, Onni!" Annika scolded.

"Uh, I mean, I've only seen him once," Mikko deflected, hoping they would lose interest. In reality, he had seen him nearly every night since moving in, and he wished his guests would leave before the nightly ritual began.

"Oh, it's a man? Never mind." Onni pouted, sat down again, opened a beer, and launched into a stream of gossip and chit-chat about their workplace. Mikko was relieved when the subject abruptly turned to other affairs. Most of them forgot the mention of the exhibitionist in the adjacent building, except Nilas. He was still curious about it and watched Mikko very closely, noticing his distraction and the frequent glances he made toward the window.

He later cornered him in the kitchen alone.

"What else did you see?" Nilas probed.

Mikko knew precisely what he was bringing up, but still tried to evade it.

"Excuse me?" he stepped back from Nilas, who was uncomfortably close. Nilas was strikingly handsome, but there was something *slutty* about him that made Mikko uneasy.

"I see how you keep glancing at that window. Something must have really caught your attention. So what was it?" Nilas pushed on.

"Why do you need to know?" Mikko pushed back defensively.

Nilas looked him up and down and leaned in closer, whispering in Mikko's ear.

"Are you a voyeur, Mikko?"

Mikko felt the heat rising. His neck flushed, then his cheeks.

"What? No…No, I'm not like that," Mikko flustered.

Nilas took a lock of Mikko's dark chestnut hair and gently twisted it around his finger.

"I'm not judging you. I find it kinda cute. The new boy

in Tampere is not so vanilla. It doesn't bother me at all, but if I were you, I would let Kaija know which team you're on. I think she has a crush on you," Nilas smiled seductively, then exited the kitchen, leaving Mikko in a state of embarrassed confusion.

Long after everyone had left, Mikko couldn't shake off the accusation Nilas had made. 'I am not a voyeur. I'm just...curious, that's all.' He convinced himself. Mikko cleaned up the remnants of the party, furtively stealing glances at the twelve-foot wall of paned glass windows. He shut the lights and was about to head off to bed when suddenly, a light went on in the apartment across the way. Mikko stood frozen for a moment, unable to move from the spot. He could see the young man in his apartment, his perfect physique bathed in an amber glow. He knew it was wrong to look. Mikko didn't want to succumb to his compulsion, but he felt powerless to resist it. Slowly, he sat down on the sofa facing the window and watched, entranced. The man began stretching and performing ballet moves in front of a mirror. He had a pretty face framed by long blonde hair. Mikko couldn't discern if he had blue eyes, but he had the impression that he did. The man performed an elegant bow, admiring himself in the full-length mirror in his apartment. It was mesmerizing, like watching a doll in a glass case slowly twirling. If the young man shifted too far to the right of his window, Mikko would lose sight of him. The buildings stood at sharp angles, and visibility was limited to a short range before another brick corner jutted out and obstructed the view. The Tammerkoski rapids separated the structures. Nonetheless, Mikko was captivated, and tonight's show was even better than last night's.

As Mikko observed the figure in the window, he noticed the man's attention shift to something outside. Mikko stood up and leaned forward to see what he was looking at, but whatever it was remained just out of view. The man appeared shocked, or was he simply pretending to be shocked by what he was witnessing? He performed a pantomime with silent movie exaggeration. Every muscle on his bare body was clearly defined and tense in response to a stimulus that remained unseen by Mikko. The man ran his hands all over himself, caressing his skin. His long, delicate fingers seemed to move independently, as if they had a will of their own, as though they belonged not to him but to some invisible lover. He squeezed his pectorals and then roughly twisted his nipples, smiling and wincing. He could see the man's chest rise and fall, and he could almost imagine what his breathing sounded like or perhaps even his moans of pleasure. Mikko was transfixed by the performance with an audience of only one: himself. Mikko's thoughts swirled with lustful fantasies, yet he remained silent, his voice trapped in his throat. He didn't dare to touch himself. That would make it wrong; he understood that. Only his racing heart and flushed cheeks revealed his arousal as he stared. Mikko began to ponder about the pretty doll in the glass case. Why is someone so clearly starved for connection and affection all alone, engaging in these private acts? And what is it that he gazes at that inspires him? It sparked a more profound curiosity in Mikko, and as he drifted off to sleep on the sofa, he vowed to uncover the mystery.

PART II

The museum was closed on Mondays, so Mikko took his day off to explore Tampere. He was from Hanko, a peaceful, picturesque town filled with monuments to the past. This city was vibrant, and he was eager to discover everything it had to offer. He enjoyed having Mondays off as it gave him the chance to observe others at work. He studied their faces as they opened their shops, served coffee, or delivered mail. It was an unusually sunny day as he wandered through the city, taking pictures. Just a short distance from the museum complex stood the Tampere Cathedral. Kaija had mentioned that the Cathedral housed some interesting frescoes. He was about to head inside, but was suddenly distracted by a police car and ambulance speeding down the main road. Mikko followed a few people to the end of the street and overheard talk that a body had been found at the edge of the tracks beneath the Erkkilä bridge. Mikko realized he had never experienced anything like this before. Although this was a big city, it still shocked the public. A part of him wanted nothing to do with crime, yet he felt himself being drawn in. He moved closer to the group. The event felt surreal. He arrived to see officers from a crime unit taking photos. The police pushed back a growing number of onlookers. When the crowd parted, Mikko gained a clear view. His heart pounded in his chest as he absorbed the scene before him. His initial morbid curiosity quickly turned into horror and disgust as he stepped back. He saw the body, and he recognized her right away. Annika's body lay on the black, sooty snow embankment. Her eyes stared lifelessly, with her museum name tag protruding from the pocket of her bright green puffy jacket. Mikko stood there, unable to react. A wave of nausea washed over him as he noticed the bloodstains on Annika's clothes and her limp form lying there in the cold. As more people were shoved back, he was jostled and nearly knocked over. He heard people shouting and some crying. His thoughts came quickly. Should he speak to the police? He knew her but not very well, but wasn't it only last night when she and Onni were at his home? He decided he had to speak up, at least to offer whatever help he could. But before he could say anything, he saw Onni burst through the crowd; his cries of anguish broke Mikko's trance. This was too much. He tried to stay out of emotionally charged situations like this. Mikko had learned something about himself: that he was ill-equipped for it. He couldn't offer anything; he was a stranger here, and it was too late to do anything that would make a difference, he rationalized. Mikko turned away, feeling weak and ashamed of himself. Angry tears filled his eyes. His head pounded, and he felt like he might vomit as he strode away in the opposite direction. He bumped into others who were still heading to the crime scene. Then, suddenly, he felt dizzy; he fumbled with his scarf, and the last thing he saw was a man asking him if he was okay.

When he woke up, he found himself lying

on his back on a hard wooden church pew. The vaulted ceiling was adorned with a stylized pattern of angel feathers. The beams arched and met at the center, where a black serpent with bat wings coiled against a blazing red background. Something was in its mouth, and Mikko squinted but couldn't make it out. "Oh, you're awake," a man remarked as he leaned over the church pew. He appeared to be around forty years old, with coarse hair the color of rusty metal and stormy gray eyes. Mikko slowly pointed to the ceiling frescoes. "Am I in heaven or hell?" he asked, only half...joking. "That depends on you, I suppose," the man chuckled. Mikko sat up carefully, sensing the dryness in his mouth and a slight headache. "What happened to me?"

"I saw you on the street. You were a little green around the gills, and then you passed out," he informed.

" Oh…uh...how did I get here?"

"I carried you," the man smirked.

Mikko rubbed his forehead. "I…I'm so embarrassed, but thank you...for helping."

"Well, I wasn't going to leave you on the street. You might have gotten trampled by the crowd."

The man reached into his leather bag and opened a small bottle of orange juice. He handed it to Mikko, who took a long sip. Then, the man gently touched Mikko's cheek. It startled him, but he was still groggy, and his reflexes were too slow to pull away. "Your color is coming back," he smiled.

Mikko still felt somewhat dazed and tried to sit up straighter despite feeling miserable.

"My name is Runar Virtanen. I'm the new pastor here at Tampere Cathedral," the man introduced himself, waiting for Mikko to do the same. Still in shock, Mikko let his manners slip. Instead of making a proper introduction, he launched into a confused dialogue.

"I... I've seen something terrible... I need to talk to the police... " Mikko mumbled.

"Did you see the…?" Runar gasped.

"No, no, I didn't see the murder…But I know her… They might want to ask me questions..." Mikko trailed off.

"Easy, easy, calm down. My goodness, you were friends with the girl?" Runar asked.

"Yes, well, no… I mean, Annika and her boyfriend, Onni, were at my place just last night," Mikko rushed to explain.

"Oh, I'm so sorry. How long have you been friends?"

"Not long at all; I just met them. We work together at the Vapriikki Museum. I'm from Hanko, so I don't know many people around here," Mikko clarified.

"I see," Runar said, rubbing his chin and appearing to think deeply.

"What are you thinking?" Mikko asked anxiously.

"Well, after they left your apartment, was there anyone with you who could confirm that you were home for the rest of the night?"

"No… I was alone," Mikko replied softly.

"Hmmm, the police will want to know exactly what you did after the couple left. Can you tell them?" Runar pressed. Mikko thought back to last night. He recalled very well what he had been doing, and his face flushed with shame.

"I'm sorry, I just don't remember," Mikko stammered. Runar's rather stern face broke into a strange smile.

"No worries, young man. This isn't a confessional. You should just let the police do their job. If they need to speak with you, I'm sure they will make an effort, but if I were you, I wouldn't be in a rush to do so," Runar advised.

"Why?" Mikko asked.

"Sometimes, when you're an unfamiliar face, a stranger in a town like I am, people tend to be, you know...suspicious," Runar suggested.

He stood up and offered his hand to help Mikko to his feet. Mikko gratefully accepted it, and he felt slightly better. After talking with Mr. Virtanen, he felt a sense of solace. 'That's what pastors do best,' he thought.

"Mr. Virtanen, you have been very kind. I'm sorry I troubled you, but I've taken up enough of your time," Mikko announced.

"No trouble at all. Will you allow me one more kindness?" Runar requested. Mikko couldn't imagine what Mr. Virtanen had in mind, but he felt it would be rude to say no. "Uhm... I suppose," he said.

"Have you eaten anything today?" he asked.

"No, sir, I haven't," Mikko responded, feeling like a child in this man's presence.

"I would like to take you to lunch at a place right up the street called Rioni. It is a pretty good restaurant for a small city like Tampere," Runar remarked.

Mikko chuckled, "You must be from Helsinki. For me, Tampere is a huge city."

"I am from Helsinki. You're absolutely right, my handsome young man from Hanko, who still hasn't revealed his name," Runar laughed.

"Oh, I'm so sorry. My name is Mikko Laine," he replied.

"Well, Mikko, it's all about perspective. It might be the same object, but the view looks totally different depending on your position."

PART III

The following day, Mikko woke up feeling terrible. He had slept fitfully, haunted by dreams of blood on snow and Annika's lifeless eyes. His mind played cruel tricks, replaying the scene and transforming it into more grotesque and gruesome versions as if the shock of seeing Annika like that hadn't been enough. His lunch with Pastor Virtanen helped Mikko cope with the tragic events of the previous morning. He was grateful for the pastor's assistance and emotional support. The pastor also offered him solid advice regarding the police: 'Just wait, let them do their job.' Mikko understood they would eventually come to ask him questions; it was inevitable, but he hoped they wouldn't dig too deep. As he was getting ready for work, he noticed something unusual. A small pink envelope peeked out from under his apartment door. He speculated it could be from the maintenance staff or the building manager. Mikko picked up the envelope. It was sealed with no writing on the outside. He opened it carefully and pulled out a single sheet of paper. The note was typed and had no signature.

I really like you.

That was it, just one line. Mikko immediately assumed it was from Kaija since Nilas had mentioned that she liked him. He glanced at the clock, let out a deep sigh, and tossed the note into a drawer before hastily getting ready for work.

When he arrived at work, he checked the roster and noticed many callouts—probably Annika's friends. Kaija and Onni were on the list. He thought about calling them to see how they were doing, but decided against it.

"That can wait," he said aloud.

He sat at his desk and flicked on the monitors. The blue glow in the dimly lit room felt comforting. He began reassigning security to different areas and making do with whoever showed up. There was an email regarding grief counseling if anyone needed it. Mikko sorted through some of his older emails and deleted the outdated ones. He thought back to the note under his door. There was something about it that didn't add up. 'When was it put there?' It couldn't have been last night; he would have noticed it. Even in the morning, it didn't make sense because someone who is grieving wouldn't do something like that. 'Would they?' He frowned, suddenly realizing his assumption was all wrong. It wasn't Kaija who had left the note. While he sat there, perplexed, he glanced at the monitors and noticed Nilas on camera 2 heading up the hallway. Mikko greeted him at the door, and they made their way to his desk.

"I knew you'd be here today," Nilas said as he dragged a chair over to sit beside him.

"Well, I didn't really..." Mikko stammered.

"Oh, I know. You don't have to make an excuse," Nilas patted him on the back.

"Why are you here? Weren't you friends with them?" Mikko asked.

Nilas shrugged and slowly spun around in the office chair.

"The police are questioning Onni," he said.

Mikko bristled at the mention of the police.

"Why? Do they suspect him?" Mikko tried to steady his voice.

"They might. After we left your apartment, Annika and Onni wanted to go to a wine bar on Huhtimäenkatu. I was tired, so I went home. Someone at the bar said they got into an argument. Onni left before Annika," Nilas reported.

"Argument?" Mikko repeated.

Nilas kept spinning slowly in the office chair while clicking a pen loudly, becoming increasingly annoying, but Mikko was too polite to ask him to stop.

"They argued frequently. Onni was a habitual cheater. That isn’t going to look good to the police," Nilas shook his head.

"You don't suspect him, do you?" Mikko asked.

"No, not at all. He may be a womanizer, but he's not a killer. However, the police can be lazy. They choose the easiest path. Have they questioned you yet?"

"No, no..." Mikko shook his head.

Nilas moved closer to him.

"You know..." Nilas mused, studying Mikko's worried expression. "They might question everyone who was at your place to see if they noticed anything suspicious." He paused, then asked carefully, "Did something happen that night? Was there anything unusual after we all left?"

"No... I was alone," Mikko confirmed.

"So was I." Nilas gazed at him expectantly.

Nilas leaned closer, his knees brushing against Mikko's

"Do you know what that means, Mikko?" Nilas asked.

Mikko shook his head.

"It means we don't have any alibis," Nilas announced

"Oh, I see," Mikko whispered.

Nilas stood up and walked around the small office, passing behind Mikko's chair and lightly running his hand over Mikko's shoulders as he glided by.

"Maybe we should say we spent the night together?" Mikko suggested.

Nilas's eyes flickered at Mikko's proposal to lie.

"Hmm, I don't know. Lying to the police is risky."

"It would give us an alibi," Mikko said.

"You're right. It would." Nilas considered the idea for a moment, then nodded slowly. "Okay, sure. We spent the night together. At your place. All night long." He gave

Mikko a small, reassuring smile. "Just stick to the story, and we'll be fine."

"We should agree on some details and get our story straight," Mikko advised.

"Alright, let's practice." Nilas began,

"What time did I supposedly arrive at your place that night?" He crossed his arms, waiting for Mikko's response. "And what were we doing all night? Just sleeping or...?" Nilas raised an eyebrow suggestively.

Mikko blushed. "I think we should say that you... we... we had sex," he stammered.

"Mikko, sweet Jesus!" Nilas burst into laughter. "Look at you turning red just saying those words. It's adorable." He leaned in closer, his voice dropping to a playful whisper. "But okay, for our story...after everyone else left, I came over around 9 pm, and we had sex." Nilas paced back and forth, the blue lights from the monitors casting an eerie glow on his already pale skin.

"If Kaija finds out about this, she will be upset," Mikko expressed his concern.

"Mikko, it's just a little white lie to get us out of a sticky situation," Nilas said gently, putting a hand on Mikko's shoulder. "Kaija will get over it. Besides, it's not like we're actually a couple. It's just a story."

Mikko glanced at Nilas, questioning whether he could truly trust him, yet he found himself with little choice. He was desperate to avoid suspicion.

When Nilas saw Mikko's expression, He slightly misinterpreted it. He assumed Mikko was just nervous about lying rather than doubting his trustworthiness.

"You know what? This is actually a solid alibi. No one will suspect you if they think you were busy banging me all night." Nilas giggled.

"Yes... I suppose the police will just steer clear of that subject out of embarrassment. Besides, I have no motive to... ki... kill... Annika, I barely knew her," Mikko affirmed.

"Exactly." Nilas gave him a confident smile. "I can just see the investigator's face when we provide the lurid details." He patted Mikko's arm reassuringly. "Such a sweet boy. You're probably the last person they'd suspect." Nilas teased.

"But I'm a new person here, a stranger," Mikko argued, remembering Pastor Runar's words.

"That's actually in your favor," Nilas pointed out. Why would a stranger suddenly start murdering people they barely know? It just doesn't make sense," he said, shaking his head. "No, the police will probably be more interested in people with actual connections to her. That's unfortunate for Onni." Nilas coldly concluded. He sat next to Mikko, gazing at him. Mikko watched the monitors as more people arrived at the museum, his brow furrowed in concentration. He remained utterly unaware of Nilas's gaze. Nilas couldn't look away; there was something enigmatic about Mikko. He was an unusual-looking young man. His dark hair framed his tanned face, and his amber eyes gave him a look reminiscent of a fox or a mysterious creature from a fairy tale. His movements were fluid yet strangely awkward, like when you play a film in reverse. Mikko was taciturn, which only made Nilas more fascinated by him.

"I should come over tonight. I want to be closer to you," Nilas asserted.

Mikko didn't respond. He remained focused on the flickering screens.

"Mikko, did you hear me?" Nilas asked. He couldn't tell if Mikko was distant or simply unfeeling, so he placed his hand on his thigh to gauge his reaction.

"I heard you, but there's something I need to tell you," Mikko announced. He glanced at Nilas's hand resting on his thigh before focusing back on the monitor.

Nilas straightened, his expression shifting to one of concern. He felt genuine fear, bracing for a confession he dreaded hearing. He liked Mikko, but since he was a stranger, Nilas couldn't be sure he wasn't capable of murder.

"What is it, Mikko? You can tell me anything." He leaned forward, giving Mikko his full attention. At that moment, a knock sounded at the office door. Nilas stood up abruptly, almost toppling the chair. Mikko recognized the voice; it was Akseli, one of the museum security guards. He quickly got up and went to unlock the office door. Nilas stood up as well, not wanting to look too suspicious. Mikko let him in.

"Have a seat," Mikko offered.

Akseli waved it off and stood. He glanced at Nilas, annoyed, as if he wanted him to leave.

"Do you know Nilas from payroll?" Mikko asked.

"No, I don't think we ever met. " Akseli shook his hand and turned back to Mikko.

"Some of the men just found out about …you know... Anikka, and they asked me if they could go home," He stated.

"Well, we're already short-staffed, but it isn't too hectic today. What do you think?" Mikko asked.

"I think if we could close off some of the exhibits, we can guide the visitors to a more manageable area," Akseli suggested.

"That's a great idea. We can make better use of our limited staff," Mikko said, handing him a pad to jot down the names and the number of staff members who are going.

"I'll email HR to let them know, and I'll ensure they are paid for the day," Mikko concluded.

While Akseli noted the names, Nilas sought a casual exit. However, Mikko unexpectedly interceded at the door. He embraced Nilas and said in a sultry voice, "I'll see you tonight." Mikko kissed him, eliciting surprised reactions from both Akseli and Nilas. "Yeah... tonight," Nilas responded, still bewildered by Mikko's actions.

As Nilas walked down the hallway, he was still in a daze from the kiss. It was surprising and, honestly, really quite passionate. As he approached his office, he realized why Mikko did it. It was necessary to demonstrate to their coworker that they were a couple. Akseli would, of course, spread the news of the kiss, reinforcing their lie to the police. It was actually a brilliant move — bold yet genuinely clever. 'Maybe I have underestimated him,' Nilas thought. He set aside his suspicions about Mikko in favor of his growing attraction to him.

PART IV

Despite being short-staffed, the day was not a total disaster. At closing, security needed to clear all visitors from the exhibit rooms and common areas, including restrooms and the café. Mikko often found himself among the last to leave the museum. Once that was done, Mikko and his staff could go. He was heading home when he heard someone shouting his name from across the street. It was Pastor Virtanen.

"Hello, Mikko. How have you been?" Runar asked.

"I'm okay; I'm just leaving the museum," Mikko responded.

"Oh yes, I remember when we had lunch. You mentioned you worked there, but I don't recall which department," Runar said.

"I'm the manager of security," Mikko answered.

"Right, right, a good position. It can be a bit stressful, I'm sure." Runar offered.

"Yes, sometimes. Today was a bit of a struggle. There were lots of people out because, you know…" Mikko hesitated.

"Yes, understandably." Runar paused and then began again. "Mikko, you know my offer to talk is still open," he offered.

"I know... um…" Mikko stammered.

"Mikko, you seem troubled. I apologize if I'm overstepping, but when we last spoke, I sensed a deep pain within you. Please forgive me if I'm mistaken. I am a Pastor. I am here to help people overcome their internal struggles and remove the burdens that may weigh them down," Runar said.

Mikko felt his stomach twist, and he held back tears. He never spoke to anyone about his pain, nor did anyone care. He never unburdened the sadness of his life in Hanko, the tragedy that shaped his existence, and how he came here to escape it. And now, even here, his flaw has followed him. The mistakes in his creation continue to grow. The universe played a cruel trick, a masterpiece of irony laid out before him like a feast, allowing his obsession to keep consuming his heart, mind, and body. But he wasn't ready to *unburden* any of that yet.

"I'm okay, just tired." Mikko lied.

"Well, if you need me, I am at your service. You know

where to find me, Tampere Cathedral, right up the street," Runar smiled.

"Yes, I remember; thank you, goodnight. " Mikko replied.

Mikko felt the pastor's gaze on him as he walked away, and his inner dialogue complicated their brief encounter. Thoughts flooded his mind, causing his pulse to race. 'He's worried about me. I hope I didn't give him a reason to look into my background. I have a new name that should serve as a strong deterrent. But a police officer could uncover everything in seconds. Stop thinking about that; they haven't even contacted you yet,' Mikko tried to calm his nerves by taking deep breaths of the crisp night air.

As he walked home, he thought about Nilas. He was taking a significant risk by trusting him, but he didn't have much choice. He had few friends here and never expected to find himself in such a situation. He remained uncertain whether he should tell Nilas why he didn't want to speak with the police. If they searched his name, those specific issues would come up, and he didn't want to deal with that again, especially in the context of this investigation. As he approached his building, he was surprised to see Nilas waiting outside.

"Finally! Where were you? I've been here for an hour." Nilas complained, adjusting his bright red scarf.

"An hour?" Mikko looked confused.

"Let me in. I'm freezing." Nilas shivered.

"What are you doing here?" Mikko demanded.

"You told me to come see you tonight," Nilas answered. His shoulders braced against the night chill.

"That was only because I wanted Akseli to start rumors about us," Mikko stated, looking around nervously.

"Yeah, yeah, I got that part...but that kiss tells me that you might want something more," Nilas giggled.

"No, you're wrong. I don't," Mikko said flatly.

"Shut up and let me in. I bought us dinner." Nilas held up takeaway bags.

"Fine." Mikko fumbled with his keys, unlocking the door.

Nilas walked in, quickly throwing his scarf on a hook near the door.

"Take off your shoes," Mikko ordered. "I don't like shoes in the house."

"It's very nice here," Nilas remarked, removing his shoes. "Your apartment is bigger than mine."

The apartment was spacious, with windows all around and massive metal beams spanning the high ceiling. It was easy to envision this space as a factory, as many original details were preserved. Modern lighting enhanced that aesthetic while adding warmth and coziness. The bed was situated on the upper deck, offering a view of the entire apartment. Stacks of books were still piled in the corners, waiting to be organized on the tall wooden bookshelves. Nilas looked through the titles, which were mostly classics.

"Where is your apartment located?" Mikko asked.

"Why do you want to know?… So you can peep at me,

too?" Nilas laughed. Mikko shook his head, irritated by Nilas's jab. He opened the food and got out two plates.

Nilas walked up the stairs to Mikko's bedroom and peered through the windows. "You have a good view of the lakes. That's nice. Speaking of views, have you seen your little exhibitionist lately?"

Mikko let out another frustrated sigh while placing a plate in the microwave.

"Why are you so interested in that subject?" Mikko griped.

Mikko watched as the plate turned slowly in the microwave. Nilas approached from behind and gently kissed the back of his neck.

"I told you I don't mind if you're a voyeur; it turns me on." Nilas wrapped his arms around his waist. Mikko shrugged him off.

"It shouldn't. You should be repulsed by me. Besides, I'm not even attractive." Mikko said.

"No, you aren't, but there is something about you. I'm very drawn to you." Nilas played with Mikko's hair. Mikko turned to face Nilas, gazing at him with mournful, yearning eyes.

"You're really handsome; you could have anyone in Tampere...why choose me?" Mikko asked.

"I've already had everyone in Tampere," Nilas giggled."Honestly, I don't know how to describe my attraction to you. I think it's our shared secret that has brought us closer together. We should really get to know each other and ensure our stories align perfectly," Nilas said.

Mikko gave a nod of agreement.

"By the way, they released details about the murder. Did you have a chance to read it?"

"No, what did they say?" Mikko asked cautiously.

"Are you sure you want to know?" Nilas tested.

Mikko places their meal on the table. "Uhm…Maybe after we eat."

"It's not too gruesome. But it is very interesting if you are into sleuthing…" Nilas prattled on. Mikko huffed and began to eat.

"Are you into that? I saw you have a lot of Sherlock Holmes books…It's not weird, a lot of people..." Nilas continued.

"Do you ever stop talking?" Mikko shouted.

"Yes, of course, when I'm sucking cock," Nilas laughed, and Mikko flushed and coughed on his food.

"Just eat your food; it's getting cold," Mikko grumbled.

"Yes, sir."

Nilas finally eats quietly, stealing glances at Mikko from across the table. Noticing that Mikko is intentionally ignoring him, he steps up his game by rubbing his foot against Mikko's leg.

"Stop it," Mikko warned, concentrating on his food.

"No," Nilas objected. He moved his dish to the opposite side and sidled up next to Mikko.

"I think you have the wrong idea about me," Mikko said.

"Is this the part where you tell me you're not into men?" Nilas ventured.

"It's more complicated than that," Mikko stabbed at his dinner.

"Well, it wasn't complicated in the office. That felt pretty natural," Nilas purred.

"That was different," Mikko reprimanded

"Why? Because someone was watching?" Nilas bantered.

"Yes, I mean no…" Mikko hesitated.

Nilas laughs.

"There's plenty of windows in this place; someone could be watching us right now. So come on, kiss me," Nilas whined.

Mikko slowly set down his fork. His expression turned serious, almost angry, as he reflected on Nilas's words. Mikko could feel his pulse racing and his temples pounding like they had that night. But this was different; he didn't need to hold back, and there was no need for restraint. There was a brief pause before Mikko's self-control shattered like glass. Without warning, he grabbed Nilas by the hair, not gently, but with the pent-up intensity of a man who had denied himself for far too long. His mouth crashed onto Nilas, brutal and hungry. Nilas's eyes widened in surprise, but the initial shock soon gave way to pure arousal. He melted into the kiss, his arms reaching around Mikko's neck to pull him closer. With every bruising press of Mikko's lips, every punishing bite, every possessive tug of his hair, Nilas's body responded with eager submission. His breath hitched as Mikko's tongue forced its way into his mouth. Then, Mikko slowly pulled away, stealing a few more kisses before stopping entirely.

After the kiss, Mikko breathed heavily. His face flushed, and his amber eyes blazed with passion. He stared intensely at Nilas, as if daring him to react. Meanwhile, Nilas was equally breathless, his lips slightly swollen, and his cheeks pink.

Nilas tentatively brought a hand to Mikko's lips and gently touched them. There was a moment of charged silence. Nilas was left speechless as he tried to process what had just happened. His expression radiated pure bliss mixed with disbelief. Nilas was utterly enraptured, with no trace of concern...only pure, all-consuming desire reflecting in his eyes. Mikko's voice was low and roughened by emotion as he began to speak. He tightened his arms around Nilas, holding him close before murmuring, "There's something I need to tell you... Something I've never told anyone before. About me, about my past..."

Nilas reached up and covered Mikko's lips. "Shh, I don't care. It doesn't matter." Nilas whispered.

"It does matter. I don't want you to hear it from someone else," Mikko said.

"Okay, go on, tell me," Nilas replied

Mikko gathered the courage to relive his tragedy in Hanko.

"Do you see all these books?" Mikko began.

Nilas glanced around the room.

"It's hard to miss them." He gave a puzzled look.

"During my senior year of high school, I received an academic scholarship to attend university in Helsinki. At seventeen, I dreamed of living in a big city and becoming a professor of literature. As you can see, that is not what happened," Mikko said.

Nilas held his hand, noticing how distressed Mikko was becoming.

"With one mistake, I derailed my entire future and destroyed the lives of everyone around me," Mikko revealed.

Nilas listened. This confession shed light on Mikko's dark, brooding nature, yet Nilas still couldn't envision him actually harming anyone.

"Mikko, I didn't realise you had such a flair for dramatics. What could you have possibly done that was so devastating?" Nilas asked.

"I'm cursed. Afflicted with this… this obsession, a compulsion that I have no control over." Mikko squeezed his hand tightly. Hearing those words, Nilas shuddered and suddenly realized he had made a grave mistake in insisting on becoming closer to Mikko. Nilas knew himself well; he was a reckless sort, often ignoring the red flags with the men he hooked up with and frequently putting himself in risky situations. However, in light of what had happened to Annika, Nilas knew he might have fucked up…really bad this time.

Nilas wanted to pull his hand away and run, but he felt like a deer caught in the headlights, frozen in place. 'He didn't kill her; my gut is telling me that, but I've been wrong before, ' Nilas thought to himself. Mikko stared at him with those burning fox-like eyes.

"Now you're scared of me. Oh, Nilas, I'm not going to hurt you; I'm just trying to tell…" Mikko abruptly stopped speaking, and the room fell silent, interrupted by a rustling sound at his apartment door. Both froze; someone was in the building's hallway. Mikko quickly turned and rose stealthily, moving toward the door, his bare feet softly creeping closer. Through the space at the bottom of the door, he could see boots. Suddenly, an envelope slipped under the door. This time, Mikko didn't even pause to read it. He pounced on the door as quickly as he could. In his haste, he fumbled, dropping the keys.

"FUCK!" He picked them up, unlocked the door, and ran into the hallway, but the mysterious person had vanished. He returned to find Nilas holding the envelope.

"Mikko, what is going on here?" Nilas demanded.

"I don't know!" Mikko took out the other envelope and tossed it on the table.

"Someone is leaving me these. I don't know who it is," Mikko said as he ripped open the latest missive and read it aloud.

I'm watching you. Don't disappoint me.

The cryptic message felt more invasive and ominous than the previous one. Without a shred of caution, Nilas immediately began putting on his coat, wrapping his red scarf with theatrical panache.

"Get dressed! Hurry," Nilas urged.

"What are you doing?" Mikko asked, looking confused.

"We are going to find this asshole. Come on, you're wasting time!" Nilas said as he walked out into the hallway. Mikko quickly followed suit, lacing up his boots hastily, and they exited with purpose.

PART V

The evening air was crisp and biting, promising even colder weather yet to come. Delicate snowflakes fell, catching the light from the streetlamps and creating a mesmerizing sparkle. The industrial quarter transformed beneath the snowfall, its raw, unpolished beauty emerging like a sculpture. The brick buildings were illuminated by colorful lights that highlighted their bold permanence. Nilas moved swiftly along the cobblestone path leading to the bridge, while Mikko followed closely behind him.

"Are we crazy for doing this? It might be dangerous," Mikko worried.

"We are not the crazy ones. Some weirdo is stalking you, and at any other time, I would say, '*Ooh, that sounds sexy,'* because I'm an idiot when it comes to picking partners. However, there is a killer out there, and we are somewhat connected to the murder. So, are we crazy? Yes, we are crazy, but we need to figure out what is going on here," Nilas said as he examined the tracks in the light snowfall.

"Mikko, did you notice the shoes under the crack of your door?" Nilas asked.

"Yes, I saw them; they were boots, black, I think," he said.

As they stepped onto the metal bridge, the cold air nipped at their ears, and they noticed the distinctive pattern of footprints leading across the snow-covered walkway. Each imprint was oddly pristine, perfectly preserved by the thin layer of fallen snow, as if the mysterious perpetrator had just passed moments before.

"These prints are very clear, but they could belong to anyone. How do you know we are following the right person?" Mikko pointed out.

"This is our person. The boots in the hallway were Hai boots, the classic style by Nokian Footwear. I know exactly what the tread pattern looks like: triangles with slanted horizontal lines crossing through them. These boots are the originals, which are more expensive than the knock-off brands," Nilas answered.

Mikko gazed at him in admiration of his knowledge and observational skills.

"From just that quick glimpse under the door? How do you know all this?" Mikko wondered.

Nilas shrugged and smirked, "I'm gay, that's how."

They followed the footprints for about a 6-minute walk

until they became muddled with others'. Mikko and Nilas lost their direction. They found themselves at Tampere Central Square. There weren't many people milling about, but enough to confuse them.

"Now what?" Mikko asked.

Nilas looked around at the gathering. People were walking quickly to a cafe or bar, or meeting in front of the Tampere theatre. Each person had a unique purpose.

"Our alleged secret admirer is not here," Nilas concluded.

"Are you sure?" Mikko tested, his eyes still examining the crowd.

"Yes, I'm sure. Do you see how no one is looking at us? If your stalker were here, they would be acting suspiciously or, at best, stealing sneaky glances at us," Nilas explained.

"They could have gone into any of the buildings surrounding Central Square. But we can rule out some of them because it's almost 8 p.m., and some of the businesses will be closed." Mikko pointed out.

"Yes, but what is just opening now?" Nilas smiled, and his eyes went to the glowing symmetry of the Tampere theatre.

They started walking across the square toward the theater when, suddenly, a man wearing sunglasses and a scarf pulled up around his face rushed over to them. Mikko's first instinct was to protect Nilas from any danger. He stood in front, prepared to confront the masked assailant. Mikko didn't wait for him to attack. He grabbed the man's arm and twisted it.

"Stop, stop, it's me, Onni," he struggled. Onni's voice was shaky but urgent, and he blurted out, repeating, 'It's me, Onni!'

"Onni, what the fuck?" Mikko shouted. Onni pulled his arm away from Mikko and rubbed it.

Mikko and Nilas exchange a glance, their bodies slowly relaxing from the defensive stance. Onni runs a hand through his disheveled hair, his breath still coming in quick gasps. Nilas steps forward and gently guides him to a bench.

"I heard the police have been questioning you?" Nilas asked.

"Questioning? They're accusing me!" Onni shouted, looking over his shoulder.

"You need to get a lawyer," Mikko suggested.

"Oh yeah, I have one. He said the police don't have any real evidence against me, just that stupid argument we had that night. Everyone knows Annika, and I fought, but that doesn't mean I killed her." Onni ranted, his eyes wild with desperation. A police car siren is heard in the distance, causing Onni to cringe.

"Oh no, that's awful," Mikko said sympathetically.

"I'm getting paranoid. The cops keep calling me back, trying to see if I've changed my story. I have no alibi; I was alone after I left her," Onni griped.

"Well, I went back to Mikko's apartment after everyone

left. We were together…all night." Nilas says, wrapping his arm around Mikko's waist and leaning against him.

Onni blinked in surprise, taking in the sudden display of intimacy between Mikko and Nilas.

"Wait, you two...? Since when? I mean, I didn't realize Mikko was... " He hesitates, distracted by a police car slowly cruising down the street.

"There they go again. I think they're following me. I swear I didn't do anything. You guys believe me, right?" Onni pleaded.

Nilas glances at the theater entrance, a hint of impatience flickering in his eyes.

He leans forward, his arm still casually draped around Mikko's waist, and addresses Onni with a gentle but firm smile. "Onni, we believe you. But right now, we really need to go; we have tickets." He glances meaningfully at Mikko.

"Uh... yeah, sorry. Maybe we can meet tomorrow for coffee or something," Mikko said.

"Sure, if I'm not in jail," he snarked, adjusting his scarf, covering his face again. Goodnight, guys, oh, and have fun tonight," he chuckled.

Nilas dragged Mikko toward the theatre.

"Let's get into the lobby. We need to check everyone out before they go to sit down, " Nilas said.

"I feel bad for Onni," Mikko said thoughtfully.

"Don't. You don't know him like I do. He made that

poor girl suffer by cheating on her and arguing constantly. He is not a good person," Nilas stated coldly as they entered the lobby.

Mikko watched as Nilas scanned the theater crowd, his eyes quickly checking each person's footwear. His frustration and disappointment were clearly visible on his face.

"Ugh, that idiot made us lose the trail!" Nilas grumbled.

"Nilas, you're so mean. He just wanted to talk to us." Mikko said.

" Fine, if you want to talk to him, go right ahead! I was trying to help you by finding your crazy stalker. But I guess you prefer to hold Onni's hand!" Nilas exploded and stormed off in a huff.

"I didn't ask you to do this; you just ran out after the person!" Mikko shouted as he chased him through the crowded foyer. He pushed past the throng to reach Nilas, grabbing his arm and spinning him around to face him. This action drew some curious glances, but most people assumed it was just a lovers' spat. Mikko gazed into Nilas's eyes. There was a coldness there that sharply contrasted with his usual flirtatious nature; it confused Mikko, yet he found it alluring. He felt as though he was falling for Nilas, but he had a sense it could end in disaster.

"Mikko, this is important. We need to know who's behind these notes and what they really want. Is it just to scare you, or is there something more dangerous going on?" Nilas spoke, his voice firm and focused, but there was an undercurrent of concern and something more ... a hint of his deepening feelings for Mikko.

"I... I can't stand the thought of someone terrorizing you like this, Mikko."

"I understand. I'm sorry; you're right," Mikko acquiesced. However, as he listened to Nilas ramble, a glass case announcing upcoming shows hung directly behind him, catching Mikko's eye. His gaze was fixed on a poster showcasing photographs of the theater actors. There, on the poster, was the young man he had watched from his window...the one who performed privately each night. While Nilas lectured him, he simply stared in shock. It was him...he must be the one leaving the notes.

"Mikko, are you listening to me?" Nilas interrupted.

"Nilas, it's him, he's the one," Mikko pointed to the poster.

"What do you mean? The person leaving the notes? How do you know?" Nilas asked as he turned to face the poster.

"He's the exhibitionist, the one I…I watch," Mikko admitted reluctantly.

Nilas looked at the picture of the actor. He was a slight young man with flaxen blonde hair, feminine features, and striking blue eyes. Nilas felt a twinge of jealousy.

"So, while you were watching him, was he watching you?" Nilas deduced, though he wasn't entirely convinced by his theory.

"It is possible, but I never felt he was aware that I was watching him," Mikko stated.

"Could he be threatening you? Does he know something about you? Something incriminating?" Nilas asked, trying to keep his voice down. The call bell rang out, summoning the audience to their seats. As the people moved inside, Mikko took hold of Nilas's hand and led him outside.

"We need to talk," Mikko said.

T.LI

PART VI

Mikko walks across the central square, practically dragging Nilas, and heads into the nearest bar.

"I'm going to tell you something," Mikko said. "Promise not to interrupt."

He took a small booth in the back. Bright blue and pink neons glowed around them.

"If you are going to confess to murder, I'd rather not know," Nilas said, only half joking.

"Because I have horrible luck with men and I wouldn't be surprised if…" Mikko puts his hand up to Nilas's lips to silence him.

"I'm not a murderer…" Mikko took a deep breath, bracing himself for what he was about to say, "I'm a sex offender," He whispered. Nilas looked at him, his face in deep scrutiny, slowly descending into disgust.

"If you want me to stick around to hear the rest of this, you'd better start explaining right now," Nilas demanded.

Mikko began, "Well, you know I am from Hanko, right?"

"Yes, yes, I've been there. It's a quaint town, the Riviera of Finland, except nobody is rich. But yes, I'm familiar with it. Go on," Nilas motioned to the waiter and ordered Lonkero drinks.

"When I was seventeen, I had a crush on one of my classmates. We weren't friends in school, and I would never have dared to tell him how I felt about him. He lived down the road from where I lived, and sometimes, very late at night, I would sneak out and look at him sleeping. I would go earlier occasionally, and he would be doing homework or exercising. It felt incredibly peaceful to see him in his own home, going about his ordinary tasks. It made me feel so close to him. But one night, I don't know why, I…I just started touching myself while I watched him. I reached into my pants and touched…" Mikko shakes his head as if to rid himself of the memory. "I did it three times. I wasn't only reaching in, I was fully exposed." Mikko stopped and gulped his drink. Nilas listened but couldn't help but interrupt, "You got caught?"

"Yes," Mikko said.

"But if you can believe that wasn't the worst of it," Mikko added, finishing his drink.

"I can only imagine what followed: the gossip, the shunning, and the public shame. It all must have been devastating for you," Nilas said and ordered another round.

"Since I was underage, I was sentenced to community service. Oh, and to make it even more sordid, I didn't know his little brother was also in the room; I couldn't see him from where I was standing, and the family's attorney wanted a stiffer sentence because... because..." Mikko doesn't finish.

"Sssh, I get it. You don't have to explain. Oh, Mikko, that is bad, really bad." Nilas empathized.

"That one incident created a ripple effect that destroyed everything in its path. As you can imagine, my parents were livid. They argued and blamed each other for how I turned out. Eventually, they got divorced. My father... my..." Mikko tears up, choking on his words.

"Shh, babe, it's okay," Nilas says. He gets up and sits next to Mikko, holding him as he sobs.

"We owned a restaurant…" Mikko stammered through his tears. Unable to speak further, he just made a gesture with his hand to indicate that the business had closed. It had suffered severely as a result of the scandal, and then it was done...finished.

"People in town would say, look, that's the man who raised a pervert," Mikko sobbed, drawing some attention from customers in the bar. Nilas looked around, a little concerned by the commotion Mikko was creating.

"Mikko, let's go home. Too much has happened tonight, and this is a lot to unload in public," he whispered.

"But I have to tell you! I have to let you know…I'm not a good person, Nilas, I'm not," Mikko insisted.

"Stop it! You were a kid. Kids do stupid things, especially kids like us. The world can never understand what we go through," Nilas hissed, leading Mikko out.

"Nilas, you are not like me," Mikko mumbled.

"How do you know what I'm like?" Nilas challenged.

Mikko hung onto Nilas as they walked. He wasn't exactly drunk, but he felt weak, and walking was difficult. Mikko inhaled the cold air, feeling slightly better. When they got back to his apartment, Nilas kicked off his shoes and knelt to untie Mikko's boots. They didn't speak and barely made eye contact. The weight of Mikko's confession hung in the air, creating a tense rigidity but, oddly, a newfound intimacy between them. Mikko looked down at Nilas, his expression unreadable. He allowed Nilas to untie his boots, and his rough hands rested on Nilas's shoulders for support. The simple act of removing his shoes became charged with unspoken emotions.

Nilas pulled them off slowly; his touch was gentle. Mikko watched him, and suddenly his expression darkened. Without warning, he spreads his legs, trapping Nilas on either side. Nilas looked up, his eyes wide as he was suddenly caged between Mikko's muscular thighs. Nilas gasped, his hands instinctively moving to grip Mikko's knees. Mikko reached down, his hands tangling in Nilas's fine brown hair as he forced his head back. Mikko paused, his gaze roaming over Nilas's face ... the long lashes, the full lips slightly parted, the delicate neck exposed. He admired the contrast of his tanned, sizable hand against this fragile beauty kneeling at his mercy. His thumb caressed Nilas's cheek softly.

"Beautiful.." Mikko whispered.

He watches Nilas's Adam's apple bob as he swallows hard, those full lips parted like an invitation. Nilas, on his knees, looked up at Mikko's strained face. He can easily read the unspoken need, the tightly coiled control. His slender fingers go to Mikko's belt slowly, unbuckling it. He unzipped his jeans carefully, freeing Mikko's throbbing erection without any hesitation. Nilas looks at Mikko's length, licking his lips unconsciously.

"Damn," Nilas whispered, wrapping one hand around the base. He looks up at Mikko and sees his tight jaw and stiff body. Nilas is well aware that Mikko has demons; he knows Mikko thinks of himself as unlovable. Mikko flinched as Nilas gripped him; a weak "Wait... No... don't" escaped Mikko's lips. His hands twitched, unsure whether to push Nilas away or pull him closer. Years of self-loathing screamed at him to stop this, to protect Nilas. Nilas ignores Mikko's protest, instead leaning forward and running his tongue along the underside of Mikko's cock, from base to tip. He doesn't stop to let Mikko argue, instead taking the head into his mouth and sucking firmly, as if daring Mikko to push him away physically. Nilas takes more of Mikko's length. His head bobbed faster, one hand cupping Mikko's heavy balls gently. He again ignored

Mikko's "Don't...You shouldn't." Instead, he took him deep, nearly choking. A harsh groan broke through Mikko's lips as Nilas took him deeper, the tight heat almost painful. "Fuck... stop…" Mikko choked, his hips twitching forward, betraying his protests. Mikko's breath came in ragged, uneven gasps, his body torn between two extremes. One part of him wanted to freely thrust into Nilas's mouth, to take the pleasure he so desperately needed. The other part screamed at him to stop, to push Nilas away before he ruined him with his darkness. Mikko leaned against the cold wall of his apartment, his head thrown back in silent ecstasy. His hips moved in small, desperate thrusts, matching the rhythm of Nilas's sucking. One hand grips the back of his neck tightly, as if trying to hold himself back from completely losing control. Nilas tightened his lips around the shaft, feeling every vein pulsating as he slid it in and out of his mouth. Mikko's fingers slowly raked through Nilas's hair, gently tugging as he sucked. It was a gentle, uncertain gesture, one that seemed to pull Nilas closer rather than push him away. Mikko felt the telltale tingling at the base of his spine, his climax suddenly rushing towards him, bathed in heat.

"Stop...mmngh gonna cum," he managed to grunt out, his fingers tightening almost desperately in Nilas's hair. Nilas hears Mikko's warning, but instead of stopping, he doubles his efforts. Moaning and taking him deeper. He wants to swallow every drop to prove to Mikko that he doesn't care about his past and that he desires him in spite of it. Nilas looks up at Mikko's face, eyes watering from taking him so deep. His expression says it all ... 'I know you think you're fucked up, but I want you anyway. Every dark inch of you.' He hollowed his cheeks, sucking harder as Mikko's body tensed. Mikko's orgasm hit him hard, his body convulsing as he spilled into Nilas's mouth. He bit his lip to suppress a cry, but it was too much. Tears welled up in his eyes, blurring his vision as he looked down at Nilas. Mikko's chest heaved as he tried to catch his breath, his eyes glistening with unshed tears. The sudden tenderness from Nilas is almost too much for him to bear. He hasn't felt this kind of intimacy, this kind of acceptance, in what feels like a lifetime. Nilas wiped his mouth and turned away, getting to his feet and heading into the bathroom without a word. Mikko stands outside the door of the bathroom, unsure of what to say. Inside, Nilas washes out his mouth and looks at himself in the mirror. "You've done it again, you stupid slut." he whispered. Then he put on his usual handsome grin and walked out.

"Okay, Mikko. Uh…that was fun, right?" Nilas said, nervously laughing.

"Well, I'll see you at work," he said, reaching for his coat.

"Wait...C...can you...stay?" Mikko asked timidly.

"Stay?" Nilas is stunned.

"Just hold me for a few minutes?" Mikko said. The words come out rough, awkward, as if they're strangling in his throat. His voice cracks slightly, betraying the emotional storm inside him. "'Please?"

Nilas's eyebrows furrow slightly, taken aback by the request. 'Hold me?' He's used to rolling over and lighting a cigarette after, not being asked to stay and cuddle. But there's something about Mikko's broken, pleading tone that makes him pull him into his arms. Mikko melts into Nilas's embrace, feeling a sense of peace and security he's never known. They lay on the sofa, Nilas's arms wrapped around him, pulling him close until their bodies were pressed together from chest to toe. Mikko pulled a blanket over them. They remained entwined and silent as the night wore on.

PART VII

It was a bright morning as staff arrived at the museum. It was Kaija's first day back since Annika's death, and she was already finding it difficult to regulate her emotions. Kaija stood outside the cafe where Mikko usually got his morning coffee. She took long drags on her cigarette, squinting at figures as they walked up the street. Kaija checked her watch, assuming Mikko was late or maybe not coming in at all; she angrily stomped out her cigarette as Sofia approached.

"Hey, Kaija, are you okay?" Sofia asked.

Her response was terse, "Yeah, fine."

"You don't seem fine, do you want to talk?" Sofia offered.

"No, not really," Kaija snapped.

Sofia knew well enough to leave it. Kaija had a bad

temper. When she was in a mood, she could tear your head off with her words alone.

"Okay, well, see you inside," Sofia said as she walked away.

"Wait! Sofia, have you spoken to Onni?" Kaija questioned.

Sofia turned around,

"Onni? No, I haven't. Why?" She comes closer, lowering her voice to a whisper."You spoke with him? Did he say something about…"

"No, no...nothing about Annika. Never mind, let's go." Kaija linked arms with Sofia and briskly headed to the museum.

As the girls entered Vapriikki's courtyard, Kaija spotted Mikko and Nilas sauntering up to the main entrance. They strolled with a casual intimacy, their shoulders occasionally brushing against each other. Nilas offered Mikko a bite of his Korvapuusti. A dusting of cinnamon clung to Mikko's lips. With a soft giggle, Nilas reached up to gently wipe it away with his thumb, his touch lingering for a fleeting moment.

Kaija watched them, her expression turning to rage. Sofia was surprised to see Mikko and Nilas together, but she quickly understood why Kaija was so angry.

"Oh..I didn't know Mikko was..." Sofia noted.

"He's not! It's Nilas, I'm sure he...he must have forced him!" Kaija exclaimed.

"Uhm…he doesn't look like he's being forced," Sofia

gently tried to reason with her.

Nilas spotted Kaija at the museum's main doors and guided Mikko to a different entrance. Kaija thwarted his evasive efforts and gave chase. Sofia bolted after her,

"Oh my God! Kaija, don't make a scene!"

Kaija stopped a few feet behind Nilas and Mikko. Nilas turned to face her. He stared her down defiantly, ready for the confrontation. Mikko's shoulders tensed, anticipating the verbal assault. Kaija stepped up and leaned in close to Nilas, her voice low and malicious.

"Wow, Nilas, I must say I'm impressed. It didn't even take you a week to sink your claws into Mikko. That's a new record, even for a slut like you."

Nilas's eyes narrowed, a flicker of anger igniting within their depths at Kaija's biting words. His jaw tightened, and his expression shifted from annoyance to a darker, more defensive tone.

"And what's it to you, Kaija?" he retorted, his voice laced with a dismissive edge.

"Just leave us alone." He leaned closer to Mikko, looking up at him, silently pleading for solidarity.

Mikko tried to mediate, clearing his throat nervously before he spoke,

"Hey, come on, Kaija, this is not the place to do this…"

He hadn't anticipated the situation escalating into such a drama. The initial group of onlookers had swelled into a significant assembly of his colleagues. A knot tightened in Mikko's stomach as he surveyed the crowd. The usual hum of the workplace had been replaced by an expectant hush, all eyes fixed on the unfolding scene. He recognized several faces from different departments, individuals who likely wouldn't normally cross his path during the workday, now drawn by the spectacle. It was clear that the word had traveled fast. Akseli and Onni, true to their predictable nature, had wasted no time in spreading office gossip about his relationship with Nilas. Mikko reminded himself, 'But wasn't that the plan?' All this was just to avoid a thorough police investigation because *he* had something to hide. He felt guilty and horribly selfish for dragging Nilas into this.

Kaija scoffed, her arms crossing defiantly over her chest. A sardonic smile played on her lips as she leveled a sharp gaze at Nilas.

"Us? Oh, so now you're an actual couple, I see," she sneered, her voice dripping with sarcasm. "So this isn't just some random fuck for you then?" The question hung in the air, heavy with implication and judgment, followed by an audible gasp from the stunned staff.

"Kaija, please stop. That's too harsh," Mikko whispered, appearing on the verge of tears. "Don't do this, don't..." His voice wavered slightly, but his tone was firm, putting an end to the argument. Hearing Mikko's words seemed to break Kaija from her fit. She regained composure as Sofia guided her away. With his head down, Mikko strode off, followed by Nilas. He opened the door to his office and silently turned on the surveillance monitors, keeping his gaze averted.

"Mikko…Mikko, look at me. Don't worry about her. She will get over it." Nilas began.

"It's already started…" Mikko grumbled.

"What do you mean?" Nilas followed Mikko around as he fussed over wires and repositioned computer screens, doing anything to keep himself busy.

"Nilas," Mikko whispered, his voice full of remorse, pulling him into a tight embrace. "It's my curse, Nilas. Anyone who gets close to me always ends up suffering. I just…I can't believe she made such a scene, right there in front of everyone. I am so, so sorry." He held Nilas tighter, his shame clear.

Nilas, though surprised by Mikko's intense reaction and apology, stood firm. Pulling back slightly from the hug, he met Mikko's gaze. "You are not cursed! And…I'm not scared of her, Mikko," he stated clearly, his voice unwavering. "I honestly don't care what she says about me." His expression conveyed a sober defiance and a steadfastness that contrasted with Mikko's distress.

"You're forgetting she's in HR; she could start building a case against us, try to get us fired," Mikko hissed, his voice laced with panic. His eyes darted nervously around the small office, as if the very walls had ears. "Nilas, I can't lose this job! My stepfather will kill me!" The last sentence tumbled out in a desperate whisper

"No one is getting fired…We haven't done anything wrong!" Nilas looked directly at him, ensuring he understood."Now calm down and get to work. I am going to my office, and I'll do the same, just carry on like it didn't even happen, okay?" Nilas finished.

Mikko found some strength in Nilas's reassuring words. He pulled himself together and nodded emphatically as Nilas walked away.

"Yeah… yeah…okay. Wait, don't leave yet," Mikko said as he met him at the door. He leaned in and kissed Nilas. It was different from the first time he had kissed him. This time, there was a quiet tenderness in his actions, a gentle affirmation of their bond.

Nilas closed his eyes in Mikko's embrace. 'I could get used to this,' he thought.

"I'll see you at lunch." Nilas smiled back at Mikko as he walked out.

PART VIII

Mikko sat in his windowless office surrounded by machinery. He could watch the museum's activity through the monitors. The weather had blurred over the exterior cameras, but Mikko could still see that a wet, snowy mixture was steadily falling outside. 'Nothing new there, ' he thought. He turned his attention to the interior surveillance. His primary focus was always on the security spots and his staff. Making sure everyone was in their designated areas and paying attention to the visitors passing through the exhibits. Corridors and exit doors were monitored but not manned. The gift shop also had cameras. While patrons wandered through, Sofia ignored them, busy texting on her phone. She was undoubtedly recounting the morning fireworks to one of her friends. All the other offices were out of camera view. Mikko smiled, wishing he could watch Nilas at work. He had grown accustomed to hearing his incessant chatter and biting digs at everyone. He was actually looking forward to seeing him at lunch, even though it would likely create more gossip.

'Well, great work, team, on making a lie a reality.' Mikko mused, feeling somewhat less worried about the drama he was now completely embroiled in.

In another office, Nilas set about his work with no further concerns about the earlier incident or Kaija's affront. Nilas had developed a thick skin throughout his years. Being taunted, teased, ridiculed, or reviled for his homosexuality was nothing new to him. He had been fighting that battle since he was twelve, and now, at twenty-eight, insults have little effect on him emotionally. He thought about how Mikko defended him with such chivalry and how diplomatically he dealt with crazy Kaija. He even went so far as to tell himself that they make a good couple. 'He's quiet and controlled, and I'm…well, I'm… never mind,' he was daydreaming about Mikko like a smitten high schooler when the office phone rang, interrupting his thoughts with a sudden jolt. It was an outside number, so he had to put on his *professional* voice.

"Hello, you have reached payroll. This is Nilas Niemi. How may I help you?"

There was a short, silent pause, but he could hear someone breathing on the other end.

"Hello?" Nilas repeated, already getting impatient.

"Oh, I'm sorry, I think I called the wrong department, "

the voice said. It had a deep timbre and richness to it that caught Nilas off guard. "It's fine, what department were you looking for? Maybe I can connect you?" Nilas offered.

"Well, actually, I'm not sure with whom I should speak. Yesterday, my colleague visited the museum to do grief counseling with some of your staff," the man explained.

" Oh yes…and?" Nilas waited.

"Right, well, he can't make it there today. I will be taking his place. I didn't know if I needed to get a new visitor pass or perhaps I could just use the one issued yesterday?"

"That sounds like a question for security. I can connect you to that department." Nilas said.

"Of course, I should have thought of that, my apologies," the man agreed.

"Not a problem, I can connect you with Mikko," Nilas giggled at his loss of appropriateness, "I mean, the security department."

"Thank you so much, you have been very helpful, what was your name again?" the voice on the other end asked.

" Nilas Niemi and yours?"

" Pastor Runar Virtanen,"

Over in the HR department, Kaija was considering going home after her shootout with Nilas. It didn't go the way she planned, but then again, what sort of outcome was she expecting? Perhaps she wasn't emotionally ready to return to work so soon after Annika's murder. When she closed her eyes, she replayed the argument in her head.

Mikko's expression was etched in her memory, showing hurt and disappointment toward her. It made her feel sick to think about it. 'He probably hates me now,' she thought, fighting back tears. When Mikko started working at Vapriikki, she was excited to see someone her age. Most of the people at the museum were older; only a handful were still in their twenties, and almost all were women. When she received Mikko's CV, she noticed that he had some surprisingly solid references but relatively little work experience. Kaija hired him regardless. During his training, she noted all his peculiar nuances. Most people would say he wasn't conventionally handsome, but there was something oddly attractive about him, well, at least to her anyway. Mikko spoke softly, which made you lean in closer to catch his words. His golden eyes held the summer sunshine even on the coldest day. When he smiled, it didn't quite reach his eyes; they retained that profound sadness Kaija believed she could fix. Mikko's stance at rest was a perfect example of contrapposto, like that of classical ancient statues. His scent was intoxicating, like the aroma of burning luktegress. Mikko's presence even rekindled her creative side. She began writing poems inspired by him; in short, she became obsessed with everything about Mikko. So no one can understand how much this hurt her. She was beginning to regret her morning outburst. She considered making amends with Mikko, but there was no way in Hell she was going to apologize to Nilas. He deserved it. In fact, the more she thought about Nilas, the angrier she became. He was a classic troublemaker, bringing out the worst in everyone. It seemed like Annika and Onni always argued whenever he was around. He would instigate it with a perfectly timed snide remark, a rolling of his eyes, or a sardonic chuckle. He would empathize with Annika when she suspected Onni of cheating, but then turned around and sided with Onni when it suited him.

She wouldn't be surprised if he were the reason they argued the night of Annika's murder. Kaija wondered if the detectives even questioned Nilas. They had spoken with her only briefly, but were coming down hard on Onni. He still hadn't returned to work, and Kaija realized he may never come back. So many thoughts were going through her head, leading her down dark roads. 'Different choices each have their own set of outcomes, the consequences of the decisions we make.' Kaija contemplated. She wished she hadn't gone home early that night; things would have turned out differently.

PART IX

"Hello, you have reached the Security Operations Department. How can I assist?" Mikko waited for a response.

"Mikko?"

Upon hearing that single word, Mikko recognized the voice; the deep vibrato was unmistakable.

"Pastor Virtanen?" Mikko asked just to be sure.

"Yes, yes, it is me. Nice to speak with you again!" The pastor chuckled.

"Yes, sir, how may I help you?" Mikko responded.

"I am replacing a colleague for the grief counseling session. Could I use his visitor pass, or should I get a new one?" he asked.

"You're coming here?" Mikko sputtered.

" Uh..Yes, later today, sorry for the short notice." Pastor Virtanen paused. "Is there a problem?" he added.

"No…no, uh…It's fine. The security policy states that you must have your own pass. I can print one out today, not a problem," Mikko added.

"Wonderful, I will be there from 1:00 to 3:00, it's open for all. I hope you will have time to stop in so we can chat again," he said.

Mikko hesitated. He knew for sure he didn't want to participate in the group session; he had already had enough emotionally charged dialogue for one day.

"I could try to stop in if I'm not too busy, but if I should miss you, I can leave the pass with one of the members at the front desk."

"Perfect. Thank you." Virtanen ended the call.

The thought of sitting in a group with his coworkers after what had happened this morning made Mikko feel uneasy. The last time the group session was held in the cafeteria, Mikko chose to have his lunch outside the museum. Since Nilas had been distancing himself from this tragedy as well, Mikko assumed he would likely want to do the same. Mikko called the payroll department, and Nilas, recognizing the security department's extension numbers, answered on the first ring.

Nilas's voice was sweeter than usual as he answered the call. "Hey, baby, what's up?" he gushed.

"They're having grief counseling today," Mikko mumbled.

"Ugh, yes, I heard. You're not going right?" Nilas presumed.

"I'd rather not. Can we go to lunch somewhere?" Mikko asked.

"Absolutely. Pulcinella makes nice pizza, we can go there," Nilas said. Mikko felt a wave of relief wash over him as they decided to skip the grief counseling together. The thought of getting out of the building and spending time with Nilas felt like a much-needed remedy, a break from the stifling atmosphere.

"Sounds good," Mikko sighed.

At a small community theatre, Professor Maria Hakala was preparing to introduce a newcomer to their acting troupe.

"As you know, from time to time, we are gifted some talented students who are currently completing their studies in acting or stage design. This year, we are fortunate to have a young man joining us from Näty Theatre Arts, Mr. Petri Koskinen."

Petri stood up and bowed gracefully. The actors clapped and cheered.

"Now, before I give the stage over to Mr. Koskinen, I would like to say a few things. He is one of the humblest actors I have met in my long career of teaching, so I want to take a moment to brag about some of his accomplishments. When he was only 10 years old, he had a small part in a film playing a turn-of-the-century spectre," She announced with flair before Petri interrupted.

"It wasn't a speaking part, but I screamed quite a bit," Petri admitted. The group giggled. "I was hired mostly for my acrobatic abilities," he added.

"Oh yes, that brings up another of his talents, he has studied ballet and modern dance. This past month, he was an ensemble member at Tampere Theatre." Professor Hakala interjected proudly.

One of the actors in the troupe chimed in, "If he sings, that makes him a triple threat!" They laughed in unison.

"No, no, I don't sing, well, only in the shower," Petri said, smiling and flashing his bright blue eyes and impish grin, which endeared him to the members. His playful response elicited a round of laughter from the actors, lightening the mood and adding a touch of humor to the introduction. Professor Hakala looked on with adoration, then pressed on with more information.

"Well, the last thing I wanted to mention is the most important. Next week, for the Tampere Light Festival, we will still be scattered throughout the city for the window walkabout. And just like last year, you have artistic license to create your tableaux for the shop windows around town, and you may utilize our costume department. As an added treat, we have been given a spot on the stage in Koskipuisto Park. It is fantastic exposure for us, and we will be performing a short folk play that Petri has written!" she beamed and motioned for Petri to take over. There were hushed conversations amongst the actors as Petri handed out scripts. It was simply entitled The Menninkäinen. He addressed the performers.

"Before we start, I'll give a brief summation of the story. The two main characters are both tricksters from our folktales: the Menninkäinen, a gnome-like creature, and the Tulikettu, the cunning fire fox. At the start of the play, we learn that the elusive fox Tulikettu has committed an offense against an innocent boy. He steals the boy's light force, bringing misfortune to the young man. Meanwhile, the Menninkäinen named Kosta happens to be passing by and witnesses it. He strikes a deal with the woeful youth, promising to restore his luck and dignity by catching the fox, making him pay for his misdeeds, and restoring the boy's light force by gifting him the magical fur of the fox. It's a fairly simple story, but there are some twists and turns as the two tricksters try to outwit each other," Petri finished.

"What does the Menninkäinen get in return?" A young actress named Sanni questioned.

"This gnome Kosta is quite noble. The boy's sadness moves him, but there is some talk of payment in shiny trinkets and an elaborate vegetable garden," Petri teased. Sanni laughed, "I knew it! Gnomes usually don't do things for free."

"Exactly! But the story's message is about keeping your light even in the darkest times, and I feel it ties in perfectly with what the light festival is about, whether that darkness is inside of you or all around you," he explained. The group began eagerly flipping through the script, already brainstorming ideas. Suddenly, Professor Hakala asked, "Does it have a happy ending?" Petri gave a mischievous smile, "We shall see."

PART X

Around lunchtime, before Pastor Virtanen arrived at the museum, Mikko and Nilas quietly slipped out of the building unseen. Mikko entrusted security matters to Akseli, who was more than capable. Taking shelter from the cold wind behind the corner of the brick building, Mikko waited for Nilas. He watched him from a distance as he stepped out and ran a hand through his fine brown hair. Nilas looked around, searching for Mikko. This insignificant action meant so much to Mikko. There was a sense of comfort in watching Nilas stand there, knowing that someone was waiting for him. Someone wanted to be with him. As he came closer to Nilas, Mikko hesitated for a moment, considering whether to greet him with a kiss, feeling a bit worried that Nilas might find it too sentimental or childish. But to his delight, Nilas took a bold step. He reached up to Mikko's height, gently draping his arms around Mikko's neck, and gave him a tender kiss that reminded him of those heartfelt moments in romantic movies. Mikko instinctively wrapped his arms around Nilas and squeezed him tightly right there on the cobbled courtyard outside Vapprikki. He didn't care if Akseli was watching on the external surveillance camera, although the thought briefly crossed his mind. He gently pulled away from the kiss, his eyes transfixed on Nilas's perfect physiognomy.

"I...I've never had a boy...boyfriend…I mean, been in a relationship before." Mikko stammered, immediately feeling stupid, and regretting his choice of words. Nilas smiled and said, "Neither have I." It was truthful because, despite all the men he had been with, he never considered those random hook-ups as boyfriends. It had gone from casual to meaningful so quickly with Mikko, and he understood why. Nilas couldn't resist hurt, broken men with darkness running through their veins; the ones who hide their twisted desires behind shy smiles and awkward shrugs.

"Come on, my car is over here," Nilas directed.

Back at the museum, Kaija met up with Sofia in the cafeteria. They were the first to arrive for the grief counseling session. Upon seeing Pastor Virtanen walk in, Kaija turned to her friend,

"Wait, where is the guy from yesterday?

"I don't know," she responded as she scrutinized Virtanen.

"Should we leave?" Sofia asked.

"No, let's give him a chance," Kaija said.

Pastor Virtanen greeted the group warmly. He looked over the small crowd gathered in the cafeteria; it was primarily women. He scanned the group for Mikko, who was noticeably missing. Pastor Virtanen introduced himself and immediately said, "I am not going to dwell on things that cannot be changed; I am here for the living. Annika is not suffering; she has reached a place where the struggles and cruelty of this world no longer exist, and the beauty here pales in comparison to the wonders she will see beyond our realm." His voice was not loud, but it vibrated softly at a low frequency, humming into your core. "I am here to alleviate your pain," he continued. "We don't have much time, so let's get started." The session began by recognizing their raw emotions and guiding them through the stages of grief. Kaija was surprised by the pastor's approach; his words weren't filled with cheesy religious clichés.

He began, "It's okay to be angry right now. It's okay to feel outrage, disbelief, sadness, whatever you're feeling is valid," he continued. "Annika was taken from us too soon, and brutally, in fact. It was a shock to the system, and this shock is not easily processed." He paused, letting the emotion sink in. "Imagine that you are dropped in a dark place where you cannot see the exit. You will need a guide, someone who can safely escort you out of that dangerous environment. I am that guide."

There was some soft sobbing among the women, but the audience was captivated.

"My colleague may have spoken to you about the stages of grief. You need to understand that they don't come one at a time, enter the stage like actors in a play, wreak havoc on your mind, and then exit stage left. No, they are chaotic storms of emotion that we cannot control, and our grief can manifest in many different ways."

As he continued, his eyes passed over the group like a gentle breeze through tall grass.

"Some of you might have lashed out and said things you didn't mean because your emotions were running high." His words resonated with Kaija.

"I want each of you to come up here and sit in this chair." He pointed to a simple wooden chair in the center of the room.

This is called Emotional Freedom Technique. It might feel a bit... unusual at first. But trust me, it can help release pent-up emotions," he explained the simple yet effective exercise to the group. The part about the "tapping" drew a few concerned responses, but most were interested and willing.

"One by one, you'll sit in this chair and say just one sentence. Just one. It can be anything: your anger, your fears, your hopes for justice. Whatever feels most raw right now." He gestured for the first woman to step forward. She approached, her legs trembling, and walked up to the chair.

She sat down, and Pastor Virtanen gently placed his hands on her shoulders.

"Take a deep breath," he said.

She spoke softly, "I... I don't feel safe anymore." Then she increased her volume. "I don't feel SAFE!" Pastor Virtanen squeezed her shoulders, applying pressure to specific points on her collarbone. "Good," he murmured.

"Next." The second woman sat down more confidently than the last. He kneeled before her, his hands on her knees. She yelled, "We want justice for Annika!" She then took a deep breath and screamed, releasing all the pent-up frustration and anger she had been holding inside. Pastor Virtanen nodded encouragingly, tapping gently on her meridians.

"That's it, let it all out," he added. His hands moved almost automatically, tapping meridians with practiced precision as the women shouted their truths aloud.

The room was filled with raw shouting followed by Pastor Virtanen's soothing words.

Sophia leaned over to Kaija, whispering urgently, "This is getting too intense. I don't like the way he's touching them."

Kaija shook her head firmly, "No, I need this. I want to go up there." Sophia looked worried but nodded reluctantly. Pastor Virtanen's eyes locked onto Kaija as she approached. He sat her down in the chair, his hands immediately finding her shoulders. Tears streamed down her face. He began to tap her meridians firmly, his deep voice low and commanding, "Kaija... speak your truth."

Kaija's body trembled as Pastor Virtanen's fingers pressed into her pressure points. Her mind raced with unspoken words, buried anger, and hidden rage. She opened her mouth, and a guttural scream escaped her. It was filled with years of suppressed emotion. Kaija's voice was primal, like a banshee's wail. Her body convulsed, her back arched sharply. No words escaped her. Pastor Virtanen's arms wrapped around Kaija, holding her tightly, rocking her gently as she caught her breath.

His rocking motion was almost hypnotic, creating a strange sense of unity among the group. The other women began to gather closer, their breathing syncing with Kaija's and the pastor's rocking. Pastor Virtanen suddenly pressed his lips against Kaija's ear, whispering intensely, "Let it all out, my child. Every ounce of anger, every drop of pain." His hand slides from her shoulder down her arm, fingers intertwining with hers. The other women start to mimic Kaija's screams in unison. The room fills with a roar. The pastor's eyes light up intensely as he surveys the women. Pastor Virtanen joins in the crying, his deep voice resonating throughout the space. Tears stream down his face, genuine tears. Kaija suddenly stops her screaming and turns to face Pastor Virtanen directly.

"You've released it all?" he asked, his gray eyes riveted on Kaija's gaze. His thumbs gently stroked her wrists, where her pulse points fluttered rapidly. Suddenly, he pulls her hands down, pressing them against his chest over his heartbeat. His heart pounds quickly beneath her palms. The other women watch intently, some biting their lips softly. Pastor Virtanen leans in, his voice a low, hypnotic murmur, "Feel that?" He guides Kaija's hand from his chest to his stomach, pressing it firmly against his abdominal muscles. "Feel the weight of your pain inside me now. Through my body, your pain can be transformed," he says softly, his voice taking on a reverent tone. "Your anguish, your tears, and your voices in sorrow can become melodies that touch the heavens. Your suffering can be a masterpiece waiting to be born." His stormy eyes seem to hold an unspoken promise of transformation through art and worship. Kaija felt something profound within her that she had never experienced before.

T.LI

PART XI

They walk to the nearby pizza place, the crisp air filling their lungs.

"Brilliant idea, getting us out of that grief stuff." Nilas began.

"Thanks for coming with me," Mikko answered.

"My pleasure," Nilas smiled seductively, making Mikko's heart flutter.

"I feel a little guilty about missing the meeting," Mikko admitted.

Nilas sighed, "I know, me too... It's a tragedy, and unresolved, I might add, but I couldn't stomach being in the same room as Kaija. Not after that outburst this morning." Nilas huffed.

Mikko simply shrugged, not wanting to relive the embarrassment of it all.

They placed their orders. Nilas gave detailed instructions on how he wanted his pizza prepared, while Mikko just mumbled his request without even looking at the waiter.

He gazed at Mikko from across the table. Nilas gathered that there were many layers to Mikko; he just hoped he could stick with him long enough to see what lay beneath the quiet exterior.

"Yeah, I suppose everyone's on edge, not just in our workplace. It's kind of weird to think that the murderer could be any one of the people in this restaurant right now," Mikko wondered.

"Exactly! And I don't think it's an exaggeration to feel a little paranoid. By the way, we need to talk about these notes you're getting." Nilas said.

Mikko's eyes narrowed as he remembered the chase through the streets, ending abruptly at the theater. Their pizzas were placed on the table, steam rising from the surface.

"The theater..." Mikko trails off, taking a bite of his pizza.

"That little creep," Nilas complained, a hint of jealousy in his tone. Mikko's cheeks flushed slightly at the mention of the actor.

"Yeah, that guy," he muttered, trying to keep his voice casual and disinterested.

Nilas raised an eyebrow, "That guy knows you watch

him! He's playing to your compulsions." Nilas says, wiping his mouth with a napkin.

"No way. How would he know about my..." He lowered his voice and continued, "Problem." Mikko finished.

"I don't know Mikko, but we need to find out what he is up to," Nilas warned.

"You're trying to make this into a big mystery; it's not that serious." Mikko tried to skirt the subject.

"Not serious? Someone in our circle of friends was killed. Things just got serious." Nilas paused, his expression turning grim. "What if this actor is planning on targeting all of us? Annika might have been receiving these cryptic messages as well. The police are being tight-lipped about the details." Nilas speculated.

"We don't know if the actor even left the notes. But I'm pretty confident the notes, the actor, and the murder are not connected." Mikko said, trying to control the volume of his voice as he became more agitated.

"Okay, maybe I am getting ahead of myself. Let's say this actor is not the one leaving the notes. I'll admit he doesn't look the part of a violent killer either. Then explain the private little peep shows he's performing for you, there is definitely a connection there!" Nilas challenged.

"I'm not the only one who can see him, you know. Maybe he's just an exhibitionist; he's an actor after all. I don't think it has anything to do with me specifically."

Mikko continued to punch holes in all of Nilas's observations.

"An exhibitionist moves in directly across the way from a voyeur. No, no, this is no coincidence. He knows your kink. Mark my words, he is luring you into something." Nilas affirmed.

"I just looked…I didn't…I didn't do anything." Mikko whispered.

"But you wanted to, didn't you?" Nilas asked.

Mikko doesn't answer. Just thinking about Petri's performances brought those feelings back again. If he closed his eyes, he could remember everything: the thrill and rush of blood through his body, his pulse pounding, and his cock throbbing. He lowered his head, dismissing the images, and ate silently, hoping it would stop Nilas's theorizing.

Nilas picked up on this. He realized he had pushed too far.

"Hey, don't be angry. I'm just worried about you. Okay?" Nilas waited.

"Don't be worried about me," Mikko said, shaking his head.

Nilas sighed in frustration and picked at his cold pizza.

"Come on, just eat, we don't have much time," Mikko reminded him. There was a certain gruffness in his voice that made him seem like a rough character, but Nilas knew the type; he had seen it before. Under that tough exterior was a vulnerable man.

PART XII

After lunch, Nilas and Mikko returned to the workplace, but just outside the building, they were approached again by Onni.

"We need to talk," Onni demanded, his eyes narrowing on Nilas as if Mikko wasn't even there.

"About what?" Nilas asked coldly.

"You know what... I can't say it," Onni said, stealing furtive glances. "Why aren't you answering my phone calls?" he continued, desperation growing in his voice.

"I've been busy," Nilas offered, completely unbothered by Onni's tone.

"Yeah, I see what you've been busy with." Onni looked Mikko over. Nilas turned to Mikko. "Mikko, go inside. I need to talk with Onni," Nilas directed.

"Are you sure?" Mikko asked, then leaned in closer and whispered, "Will you be okay?"

"I'll be fine. Go inside, babe," Nilas said.

Mikko hesitantly walked away. Once inside, he went to his office, worried about Nilas and driven by a burning curiosity he couldn't dismiss. When he entered, Akseli stood up from the desk.

"Thanks for taking over. Anything I should know about?" Mikko asked, a bit distracted and half interested.

Akseli raised his eyebrows, "Uh, the pastor that came in today for the grief counseling session was...odd to say the least."

At the mention of Virtanen, Mikko looked intrigued.

"Odd? In what way?" he asked, hoping Akseli would elaborate, knowing his penchant for gossip. "He did some... hmm..intense, group therapy? I guess you could call it that, but the ladies seemed to like him," he chuckled.

"Really? What happened?" Mikko asked.

"You can watch it later if you want," He rolled his eyes. "Weird stuff," he repeated as he left to go on break.

He would watch that, but right now Mikko was more interested in what was happening between Nilas and Onni. He focused on the security camera at the main doors, then turned up the monitor's volume to listen in on their conversation.

"I need help. You need to give your statement to the police. Tell the detectives I'm innocent!" Onni shouted.

"I don't *need* to do anything," Nilas stated firmly.

"If you don't help me, I'll tell them everything that happened that night," Onni threatened.

"Oh, so now you want to tell the truth? No secrets? Suddenly, you're Mr. Honesty?" Nilas scoffed.

"When I tell the Police why we were arguing, you'll be on their suspect list too," Onni growled.

"You aren't going to tell them anything, and you know why? Because you've got more to lose than I do," Nilas hissed.

"You had a motive to kill Annika!" Onni screamed.

"A motive?...Really? That's rather complicated. Are you willing to explain it all to the police? Go on, what's my motive, Onni? Let me hear you say it out loud," Nilas challenged.

Onni glared at him, his face twisted in frustration.

"Yeah, I didn't think so. You're twice the coward, still can't face the truth, because if you had the balls to do what you needed to do right from the start, things might have turned out differently."

Nilas turned away and headed back inside the museum.

After hearing this, Mikko became suspicious. 'What is he mixed up in?'

When Mikko recalled asking Nilas to be his alibi, Nilas agreed rather quickly. Now Mikko started to wonder, 'Did he need an alibi more than I did?'

. . .

Over in the HR department, Kaija was still processing the session with Pastor Virtanen.

Sitting at her desk, she closed her eyes, and she could still feel his strong hands on her body. She flushed from the thought of it.

"Kaija? Kaija? Are you okay?" It was Sofia. She had left the session early, but was still curious to know how it went.

"Yeah, I'm fine," Kaija responded, breaking out of her daydream.

"Sofia, you should have stayed! Pastor Virtanen was amazing. The whole group session was... transforming." She beamed.

"I'm not into that sort of stuff," Sofia confessed.

"I feel so much lighter. Like a burden was lifted." Kaija closed her eyes, trying to recall the feeling, a soft smile playing on her lips.

Sofia sat down on the edge of Kaija's desk, her brow furrowed with concern. "Are you sure? He seemed very intense. And those methods…were a bit much," Sofia frowned.

Kaija looked up at Sofia, her gaze clear. "It was intense…but in a good way. I feel like he helped me release so much pent-up tension." She said.

"I don't know…You didn't find it… weird?" Sofia shivered slightly, despite the office's warmth.

"It wasn't the kind of speeches that you usually hear from Pastors. He understands stress and emotional pain.

Pastor Virtanen didn't even know Annika, but it was like he could feel how much we miss her and our collective outrage at her murder," She paused. "Pastor Virtanen is a healer, in every sense of the word." Kaija's voice was full of conviction. "It was like he was physically drawing the negativity out of me."

Sofia looked skeptical. "And you believe that? That he 'drew it out' with his hands?"

"I haven't felt this peaceful in years. You know, I was feeling so guilty about what I did this morning. That anger that I felt towards Nilas… I was enraged, but now I understand where that was coming from." Kaija's face glowed with a newfound radiance.

"You were definitely out of control. I tried to stop you but…What did he say to you, specifically?" Sofia persisted, her curiosity outweighing her discomfort. Kaija leaned back in her chair, a thoughtful look on her face. "He didn't say much. He mostly listened, and then he guided me. He asked me to focus on the feelings in my body, and he would gently press on certain points, sometimes holding them for a while. He explained that emotional blockages often show up as physical tension, and by working on the physical, we can unlock the emotional."

"And he thinks he can help us deal with the murder through these sessions?" Sofia pressed.

"In just that short time, it felt like I tapped into something. It got me thinking about my actions. My tendency to overcommit, my bad temper, and the pressure I put on myself to be perfect at work. It felt like he made me see myself clearly."Kaija sighed, a contented sound.

"So, he's a mind reader now, too?" Sofia's tone was a little sharp.

Kaija chuckled softly. "No, I think he's just empathetic or intuitive. He's trained to read body language and to sense where people are holding their pain. The way he... interacted with me... it felt so safe. His hands were firm but gentle, and there was no inappropriate energy. It was purely about healing."

"Are you sure about that? Because the way you described it earlier, it sounded like you were... a little too impressed by his touch." Sofia's voice was laced with a hint of sarcasm.

Kaija's cheeks flushed slightly, but her gaze remained steady. "I was impressed by his skill. It was very effective. It's hard to explain."

Sofia looked away, a troubled expression on her face. "I just worry about you, Kaija. This whole 'spiritual healing' thing… it can get… I don't know creepy. You know you tend to get a little fixated on men who have that strong magnetism. Sometimes you overlook red flags. Look how you misjudged Mikko."

"I didn't misjudge Mikko, I underestimated Nilas!" she snapped, her fiery personality returning so quickly it startled Sofia.

"I'm not fixated. Pastor Virtanen has a genuine desire to help people. He even offered follow-up sessions, free of charge, because he saw how much I was struggling." Kaija's voice was firm.

"Okay, if you're sure, just... promise me you'll be careful. And if you feel even a little bit uncomfortable, you'll tell me, right?"

"I promise," Kaija said, her smile returning, brighter than before. "And you should really reconsider, Sofia. You have your own burdens to carry. Maybe he could help you, too." Kaija suggested. She was the only person at work who knew about Sofia's home life. Her father was out of the picture long before Sofia was even a teenager, and she took care of her sick mother on her own.

Sofia hesitated, then shook her head. "Maybe someday. But for now, I'll stick to yoga. Less hands-on." She managed a small smile.

PART XIII

It was late October, and the mood in Tampere was lively. The beginning of Valoviikot, the Festival of Light, transformed Tampere into an illuminated wonderland.

Locals and visitors packed hotels to watch the opening ceremonies and participate in all the events organized throughout the town. Plain brick facades came alive with artistic light projections. Streets were decorated with illuminated garlands. The Vapriikki Museum was right next to the Tammerkoski rapids, which were the center of the celebrations. Colorful spotlights were positioned along the bridges and banks, casting shimmering reflections on the rushing water and turning it into a rainbow.

From Mikkos' apartment, he observed the lights. He leaned against the cold glass window, his breath clouding the surface. When Mikko was a child, his family visited

Tampere during the festival, and he remembered the awe he felt as a young spectator. He never could have imagined that he would one day be living in this place, alone. He felt homesick and yearned for those days of innocence before everything changed. He texted Nilas, but he wasn't responding. Mikko recalled the conversation he overheard between Nilas and Onni. 'Something is not right,' he thought. Mikko was well aware of Nilas's reputation, and it was slowly undermining his trust in him. The more he dwelt on it, the more pissed off and jealous he became. He put on his coat. "I gotta get out of here,"

Over at the theater, the play titled "The Menninkäinen" was nearly ready for its debut. Petri Koskinen impressed his fellow actors with his portrayal of the agile and mischievous creature. His lines were often written in riddles, and at times it was unclear whether he was a helper or a hindrance to the human characters. The play kept the test audience guessing and completely captivated. In the end, the message was clear, light prevailing over darkness and good over evil. A few of the players asked Petri if he wanted to get a drink with them. He politely declined and left the theater alone. Professor Hakala caught up with him.

"Petri, a moment," Professor Hakala called out.

Petri turned, a question in his bright, blue eyes. "Yes, Professor?"

Professor Hakala walked towards him, "Can I offer you a ride?"

"No, thank you. I live nearby. Besides, I would like to

see some of the light displays, but I appreciate the offer," Petri replied.

Her brow furrowed slightly. "Okay, that's fine, but.. May I offer a word of caution, my boy. Just before you head home."

Petri waited, his expression unreadable. His delicate appearance suggested a certain fragility, but beneath the surface lay a quiet resilience.

"There was some rather distressing news. I don't know if you heard," Professor Hakala continued, lowering her voice. "A young woman was murdered. Very recently here in Tampere."

Petri’s gaze remained steady. He didn't flinch, didn't show any outward sign of alarm.

"Really?" Petri echoed, his voice soft. "That’s…unfortunate. A terrible thing." He added.

"Indeed," Professor Hakala said, studying Petri’s reaction carefully. "It’s been all over the news. The police are still investigating. They have a suspect, a young man named Onni Jaskari, but they haven't made a formal arrest yet." She paused, her eyes searching Petri’s face. "I know Tampere might seem like a safer city compared to Helsinki, but just be careful going home tonight."

Petri offered a small, almost imperceptible smile, which seemed odd to the Professor in the context of their conversation.

"I can take care of myself, but thank you for your concern." He walked off.

Petri was making his way from Keskustori Central Square outside the theater to the Tammekoski bridge that led to his apartment complex. It was a short walk, but he took his time taking in the sights. The dazzling displays drew onlookers, and couples walked hand in hand. He weaved through throngs of people.

From street stalls, a sweet aroma of Glögi and the savory Makkaraperunat mingled with the crisp air. Petri picked up both and continued along the street to his home. The trees, now almost leafless, were adorned with delicate strings of fairy lights, casting a warm glow down the path. There were fewer people as he neared the apartment building. The hum of the city sounds gave way to the rush of the rapids. Petri took a moment to enjoy the dazzling lights from this view.

Petri turned and spotted a tall man walking briskly across the bridge. He was hunched over, and his face was hidden in shadow. He appeared threatening, like a man who meant to hurt someone. But it didn't scare Petri; he stood his ground. As the distance closed between them, their eyes met. In that instant, Mikko realized it was Petri the actor.

'Keep walking, don't stop,' A voice inside Mikkos' head ordered as he averted his gaze and strode past him.

Petri, however, seemed to recognize him as well and broke the silence.

"You have a keen eye," he began, his words laced with a subtle seduction. "Did you appreciate my performance?"

Petri smiled, leaning against the railing of the bridge, his voice like tinkling chimes.

Mikko stopped, his hunched posture straightening slightly as he turned back.

'Nilas was right; that act was intended for him.' Mikko thought. 'He knows something about me, but how?'

His eyes blazed and bored into Petri's. He had expected fear, perhaps anger, but not this… invitation..this challenge. "Performance?" he echoed. Mikko's voice was a gravelly baritone that sent a shiver down Petri's spine.

Petri smiled, a slow, knowing curve of his lips. "Yes, do you like watching me?" he repeated. The wind whipped around them.

"Why me?" The simple question was all Mikko could muster. His throat was tight with his growing anxiety.

"Why not?" Petri teased, his eyes never leaving Mikko's.

Mikko took a step forward. He leaned in closer, intent on intimidating the truth out of this arrogant brat and putting an end to the game he was playing. He was so close to Petri that he could feel the heat radiating from him, but the young man remained unimpressed by Mikko's strong presence.

"Have we met before? Do you know me?" Mikko challenged.

"I know what you need," Petri's rebuttal was clear. It was the truth, but it was not the answer Mikko wanted to hear. He had needed it, wanted it, and anticipated it every night like a drug.

For years, Mikko had controlled his compulsion, but his resolve crumbled when he saw Petri. This crafty young man set a trap, and Mikko fell into it like a fox in a snare.

They stood on the bridge, caught in a silent, charged exchange. The world around them faded into a blur, their focus solely on each other and the dangerous possibilities that lay between them. The night was young, and the stage was set for a performance unlike any other.

PART XIV

Kaija and Sofia went to the opening ceremonies at Koskipuisto Park. There were several musical performances on stage, followed by a beautiful display of the Dancing Fountains. The weather was cooperating, and large crowds were enjoying the spectacular show. Sofia was having a great time, but Kaija was a bit distracted. Somehow, this year's festivities felt disjointed. Her conscience questioned whether they should be celebrating so soon after Annika's murder. The thought of her, vibrant and alive just last week, sent a shiver through Kaija. She began to obsess. 'Onni is not a killer, the police are so convinced of his guilt they aren't even bothering with anyone else! Wait…What if the actual murderer is here?' she spiraled, scanning faces in the crowd as if she could sleuth out the killer.

"I'm losing it," she muttered, fighting the urge to leave and just head home.

"What's that? I can't hear you, the music is so loud!" Sofia yelled back as she swayed to the beat. Sofia seemed oblivious to Kaija's mood shift. Across the crowd, two young men made eye contact and strolled over.

"Hey, pinkie girl, love that hair!" the ridiculously tall blonde one commented as he reached out to touch Kaija's dyed hair. He spoke in English, so she assumed he was not from Finland.

She pulled away, not in the mood for flirting. Sofia, being an excellent mediator, stood in between.

"Yeah, her hair is cute, but it's not cotton candy, so don't pick at it, okay?" She smiled to soften the comment just in case the guy took it the wrong way. The other young man stepped up.

"Sorry, he's Swedish, no manners," he joked. "I'm Niels, he's Ivar, we're interns at Tampere University Hospital."

Kaija knew they were going to ask to get a drink somewhere; she could just sense it. On any other night, she would be ready to have fun, but tonight was not the night.

"I keep hearing about this event called the window walkabout, but I don't know where it actually takes place? Do you know?" Ivar asked.

"It's sort of all over, but most of them are in the city center, not far from here." Sofia offered.

"There are art installations, and actors dress up in costumes and create themed presentations," Kaija added, trying to be informative but at the same time making it sound unappealing to the young men.

"Sounds interesting. Maybe you girls would like to be our guides? We can check them out together?" Niels suggested

"Yeah, okay," Sofia agreed, answering for both of them, assuming Kaija would be on board. Kaija was not, but she went along anyway, making her best effort. A few months ago, she would have been thrilled to meet two handsome young men, medical students no less, but her passion was somehow absent, which worried her. She felt that Annika's death was a harbinger of something more evil. First, Onni being taunted by the police, followed by her disappointment with Mikko. 'This string of events isn't the end of it,' She sensed. It was the beginning of something more calamitous on the horizon. Kaija followed along, looking at the performances behind the shop windows. It felt like her world was behind glass, and the rest was outside. Nausea took over as they neared the area where Annika's body was found. Sofia didn't even notice, just laughing with the young men. They headed up the street, and in the distance was Tampere Cathedral. She thought of Pastor Virtanen; she had felt clarity with him. He was a force that anchored her when she felt like things were falling to pieces all around her.

"Hey Sofia, I think I might go home. Im not feeling well." Kaija said softly.

"Oh no, we were going to go to Café Europa after this,"

Sofia sighed. The two young men tried to coax her to stay, but Kaija excused herself as politely as she could.

"You go, really, Im just tired." She smiled weakly and headed home.

Back on the bridge, Mikko leaned in closer to Petri. He pressed against the railing, pushing his weight against Petri's slight figure. In a hushed voice, he asked,

"What do you want from me?"

"Isn't it obvious? I want your attention," Petri answered.

"Well, you got it... You may have gotten the attention of the whole building…everyone can see you," Mikko griped.

"I don't care about everyone…just you," Petri replied.

"Stop with the riddles!" Mikko shouted.

"Riddles? Riddles are questions, and you're the one asking all the questions. I'm providing the answers and solutions. Solutions to your problem," Petri pointed out.

"I don't have a problem, but you might...you keep flashing your body like that…you're asking for trouble," Mikko warned.

"I'm an actor, I'm just rehearsing. No crime in that," Petri giggled.

"But I'm not so sure about what you are doing." Petri suddenly grabbed Mikko's arm, pulling him even closer. Mikko was surprised by Petri's strength. Then, without warning, Petri put Mikko's hand on his groin.

"You like what you see, don't you?" He pressed Mikko's hand more firmly against his cock, and Mikko could tell that this conversation was turning Petri on. He was relishing his dominance over Mikko.

"I know you've been watching me. Every night. Through those windows." He pulls back slightly, his eyes locked with Mikko's. Mikko felt as if reality had unravelled… the small semblance of his ordinary existence was shattered by this meeting. He wished that this seductive stranger were a figment of his imagination, created by shameful guilt or that unrelenting need that gnawed at the back of his optic nerve.

"And now I want something in return." Petri's voice drops to a whisper, his fingers intertwining with Mikko's as he presses his hand harder against himself.

"I could tell everyone what a dirty little voyeur you are. Or..." He leans in closer, "...I could make a deal."

Mikko wrenched his hand away from Petri's body.

"You watch me again tonight, through your window." Petri's lips brush against Mikko's ear as he speaks. "But this time, you record yourself. I want to see you getting excited, jerking off, I want to see cum dripping over your knuckles. And then you send me that video, I need to see how much you enjoy my show." His teeth gently nip at Mikko's earlobe. "Or I'll make sure everyone knows about your naughty habit."

Mikko's past resurfaced in the form of this sinister sprite. Petri used flirty, manipulative banter, making it seem like a consensual, kinky game to hide the blackmail element. And although there was no request for money, it was clearly a threat... a life-changing one.

"Come on, big boy. If you get to watch me, it's only fair I get to watch you too, am I right?"

Petri reached into Mikko's large coat pockets and grabbed his phone. He quickly added his number.

"I'll see you tonight, and make sure you give me a standing ovation for my performance, if you know what I mean…don't disappoint me." Petri winked at Mikko as he stood there, stunned. He watched Petri waltz away, his feet barely touching the glistening snow crystals underfoot.

PART XV

Kaija was relieved to get home. She settled into her comfortable chair with a cup of tea, enjoying the solitude and darkness. Her cat, Rakas, leapt onto the table and strolled across her laptop's keys. She shooed her away and was shocked to see the screen displaying a view of Tampere Cathedral. She stared at it in disbelief.

"This is a sign," she whispered.

Kaija sat down and prepared to conduct a deep dive into information on Pastor Virtanen. Rakas offered a look of disapproval. "Yeah, I'm obsessed. Big deal," She answered the judgmental creature. At first, her search yielded no results. Once she found his first name, Runar, she unearthed a bit more information. She scrolled through a few articles and images. Kaija's brow furrowed in curiosity. Pastor Runar Virtanen's resume is impressive: working in multiple churches across Finland, traveling to Asia to study meditation techniques, and showing considerable talent for painting. She paused, clicking on a few more links. In one of the photos, she noticed an unusual painting. It depicted a large wooden Viking ship adorned with white angel wings, soaring up into a stormy sky with only one shining, narrow path to the Sun. Kaija looked at the picture more closely, wondering if Pastor Virtanen had painted it. She was curious about the meaning behind the imagery but thought she couldn't ask him about it, or he would know she had searched him. On closer inspection, she noticed it was hanging in his office. If she were to visit him, she could strike up a conversation, and this artwork would be the perfect catalyst. This idea had lifted her sullen mood, but it was short-lived when she spotted an email from the police department.

Mikko had meant to find Nilas, but now he turned around, his footsteps feeling heavy as he headed back to his flat. Once inside, he could see that Petri's apartment was still unoccupied. Mikko waited, sitting in his darkened apartment. He tried a few more times to reach Nilas, texting an angry message, then deleting it. 'How pathetic would that be if Nilas was down on his knees with another man and my desperate texts came through?' He felt so alone, misunderstood, and reviled. Across the dark expanse, the lights came on in Petri's place.

"Showtime," Mikko whispered bitterly.

Mikko moved as if under a spell. He slowly undressed,

his eyes fixed on Petri's apartment. He sat on the sofa facing the wall of windows. Mikko set up his phone, the camera aimed at his body, as his hand wrapped around his cock as per Petri's demands.

Petri appeared in the window; the subtle lighting cast a warm glow on his lithe figure. Mikko watched in conflicted arousal as Petri's body undulated gracefully, spinning to some unheard melody. Petri removed his layers of garments one by one, revealing his toned form. Then his movements became more explicit. Petri straddled an oversized chair and put a pillow between his legs. It was placed strategically so he wasn't completely exposed, but his actions were so lewd that it hardly mattered. He began moving up and down on the cushion, simulating riding an invisible lover with practiced precision. Mikko could almost imagine the moans and soft gasps as if he were actually in the room. Petri's head fell back in ecstasy while Mikko observed helplessly across the way.

As Mikko forced his hand to move, memories of Juhani flooded his mind. The boy he secretly loved in high school was the reason he was eventually arrested and labeled. That same reason is why he now hides his identity. Each stroke of his cock became tangled with those forbidden feelings from years ago. Mikko's hand moved mechanically up and down his shaft, torn between revulsion and the familiar lure of his voyeuristic tendencies. He was powerless to look away, feeding off Petri's erotic display, even as shame and disgust roiled within him. Each one of Petri's motions was a cruel command Mikko couldn't disobey. This stranger had appeared out of nowhere to torment him. 'What pleasure is he getting out of my humiliation?' Mikko thought. But then he realized, he was no different. Seeking sexual gratification by secretly watching strangers. One feeds the other.

As Mikko's arousal grew, his breath hitched. His hips started to move slightly in time with his hand, seeking more friction. The memories of Juhani intensified. He remembered how he used to watch him from afar, outside his window. Just the thought of it made Mikko's cock throb painfully…it hardened against his palm, betraying him. He tried to push down the arousal, but each graceful movement of Petri's body across the way made it impossible. He struggled silently, biting his lip, trying to maintain some semblance of control…But the battle was futile. With a quiet groan, Mikko gave in, his hand moving more purposefully now. He jerked off while watching Petri's erotic ballet, the shame and arousal mixing into a toxic brew. Just as Mikko reached the peak, his eyes widened with sudden clarity. He froze, his hand still around his member, as he stared across the way at Petri. The realization hit him like a ton of bricks. He knew exactly where he'd seen that face before.

With a final, desperate gasp, Mikko cums into his hand, the bittersweet release mirroring his torn emotions. The sight of Petri, the memories of Juhani flooding his mind, and the sudden realization about their shared past - it's all too much.

Once it was over, Mikko was disgusted with himself. He wiped his hand clean and stared at the video file, his thumb hovering over the send button. He was angry at Petri for manipulating him, and at Nilas for being unavailable when he needed him. Each passing second without a response from Nilas fueled his frustration and despair. 'What will happen if I don't send him this video?' he asked himself, fully aware of the consequences. It all comes crashing down just like it did when he was seventeen, only this time it will be worse.

Mikko's voice cracked with raw, suppressed pain as he whispered to himself, 'I can't do it. I can't send this fucking video.' Tears streamed down his face, blurring the screen of his phone.

PART XVI

The next day at work, Mikko angrily stormed into Nilas's office.

"Glad to see you're alive!" Mikko growled. Others in the office turned around, shocked by the sudden disruption. They were surprised not only by this outburst but also by who it was coming from, the usually quiet young man who worked in security.

Nilas jumped up and walked him into the hallway to de-escalate the drama.

"Where the fuck were you last night?" Mikko demanded.

"I...I had to do something," Nilas stammered.

"Or someone?" Mikko accused.

"Oh come on! No...Mikko, I wouldn't…" Nilas

objected. Mikko regretted his hurtful words, seeing the pained look on Nilas's face.

"I'm sorry…I needed you…fuck!..something terrible is happening," Mikko's voice trembled.

"Are you talking about the email?" Nilas questioned.

"What? No…wait, what email?" Mikko asked, confused.

"The police want everyone who was at your apartment the night Annika was killed to come down for questioning."

"Noo..Nilas, I can't do that."

"Stop this..we have each other's back! Remember?" Nilas tried to calm Mikko.

"No, no, you don't understand...you were right... the notes... the luring me in...I'm fucked!" Mikko ran a hand through his hair.

"Wait..the actor?" Nilas asked.

"Yes…yes. Petri Koskinen, it's a stage name, but I remembered him," Mikko confirmed.

Nilas looked at Mikko, confused but desperately trying to make sense of what Mikko was babbling about.

"It's the brother…He's the one. The little brother was there… he saw me that night, he was the one who called the police on me. I must have blocked it, but now I remember."

Nilas finally made sense of it. All his suspicions were fully realized.

"He found you, and he's blackmailing you, isn't he?"

Mikko nodded, "Nilas, please help me."

"Shh shh, I'm going to... but you have to get hold of yourself...Is he asking for money? How much?"

"No, he didn't ask for money. He wanted me to...to film myself. He wants me to send this." Mikko showed him the video.

Nilas looked at the video. His face flushed with anger.

"Please tell me you didn't send this!" Nilas grumbled.

"I didn't," Mikko replied weakly.

"Mikko, this isn't blackmail, it's revenge. He's going to use this against you. He'll tell the police you're targeting him, maybe sexual harassment, who knows. He wants to see you punished as an adult, probably thinks you got off too easy back then. Retribution for his brother, I'm assuming,"

"I guess…I mean, yes, you're right…but why now? It was 7 years ago!" Mikko exclaimed.

"You covered your path pretty well, but somehow he found you. Whatever happened to this classmate of yours? The one you spied on?" Nilas questioned.

"Juhani? I don't know. We had no contact after I was arrested. I went to the juvenile corrections center and finished my high school degree there. When I got back home, I think they had moved. I never contacted anyone since then. Why?"

"I'm trying to figure out if he's putting Petri up to this, or if this is something he just decided to take upon himself?" Nilas guessed.

"Why would that matter? He's still hell bent on ruining my life," Mikko concluded.

They hear footsteps coming up the stairwell and immediately stop speaking.

"Is everything all right over here?" Akseli interrupted their meeting.

"Yeah, yeah, we're okay," Nilas responded. "Uhm, actually… Can you take over for Mikko this afternoon? I was just telling him that we have to go down to the police station. It's about Annika's case."

"Oh, sure, not a problem. You okay, Mikko?" Akseli pried.

"I'm fine. You know, uhm, police stuff… Makes me nervous," He played it off.

"Hey, don't worry, they're pretty sure they know who was responsible."

"Right," Mikko waved him off, trying to hide his reddened eyes.

"Just give me a heads up when you're leaving the building," Akseli nodded and tapped the walkie-talkie on his hip belt as he strode down the hallway. Nilas waited till Akseli was out of earshot.

"Listen, Mikko, what is the worst Petri can do to you?"

"Worst case? He can go to the police. I get arrested again. It all depends on how far he's willing to go to fuck me up. If he knows where I work, He can get me fired. I won't be able to face my mother and my stepfather. He pulled a lot of strings to get me this job. He works in security. If it gets out that he falsified my CV, he's fucked too."

"Obviously, he's been planning this for a while. It might be some kind of obsession for him, but right now, he has nothing on you. Delete that fucking video. I can't believe you even let him manipulate you like that...my big dummy," Nilas reached up and playfully smacked Mikkos' cheek.

"Don't worry, I'm going to fix this," He reassured Mikko with a tight hug.

'When you fall for troubled men, you get good at fixing problems,' Nilas thought to himself.

Kaija took a break from her desk and went to the gift shop to chat and find out what Sofia and the interns did after she left. She was also curious whether the police had emailed Sofia. When she entered the gift shop, she was surprised to see Ellie, the manager at the front counter.

"Where's Sofia?"

"I don't know, she was a no-call no-show today," Ellie complained.

That wasn't like her. Kaija knew that Sofia's mother was ill, so she immediately assumed there was some health emergency. She got out her phone.

"Ellie, she's not picking up."

"I think her phone is off. I tried calling earlier. Do you have their home phone number?" Ellie directed.

Kaija nodded as she dialed.

An unfamiliar voice answered, "Hello?"

"Is Sofia at home?" Kaija asked.

"No, she's at work. I'm the day nurse for Mrs. Korpi. Who is this?"

"I'm Kaija. We work together, but she's not here either."

"Oh… I thought Sofia went in early because she's usually here to let me in. Good thing I had my key." The nurse replied.

"Sh…she didn't come home last night?" Kaija could barely speak, her mouth suddenly dry.

"Well, that's what Mrs. Korpi said, but you know she has dementia, so I thought nothing of it. But I guess she was correct," the nurse surmised.

Kaija remained silent. Ellie stared at her with curiosity, eager to discover what had happened.

"Dear, you might want to call the police," The nurse suggested.

"Yes… yes…I will do that, oh, and if she shows up, please call me."

"Will do," the nurse ended.

Last night, she was so caught up in her own mood that she didn't even realize she left Sofia with the two men they had just met. What were their names? She desperately tried to recall, but her mind was blank. All she could remember was that they were interns at Tampere University Hospital, that is, if they were telling the truth. Could she have spent the night with one of them? No, she is not impulsive like that. But why isn't she answering her phone? Kaija panicked.

"She didn't come home last. I'm going to call the police."

Ellie looked shocked, then grabbed Kaija's hand.

"Wait, just go down there, they won't take it seriously if you call."

Kaija nodded. She returned to her office and informed her supervisor that she had to leave. She tried to hold back her emotions as she exited the building. "If something happened to her, this is my fault' she thought as she left.

During the final rehearsals of The Menninkäinen, Petri's mind kept wandering back to Mikko. He hadn't planned on their meeting happening so soon. It wasn't part of the grand design he had laid out. Petri sat in the wings waiting for his entrance as the mischievous elf. In acting, it's crucial that the timing is correct, but sometimes you need to improvise. Someone could flub a line, and the whole direction of the action can take a different twist.

"That's not going to happen," he whispered to himself.

Petri checked his messages one more time and cursed, slamming his phone down. He had expected the video by now, but there was no sign of it. Petri heard his cue and leapt on stage. His lithe figure moved gracefully, twirling and bending, embodying the character's agility. His dress was scant, almost inappropriate, consisting of carefully placed mossy cloth, twigs, and leaves found in the forest underbrush. Petri spoke his lines with a melodic voice, laced with seductive undertones and rhyming riddles. Off stage, he thought he heard the familiar *ding* of a message.

He hadn't turned off his phone notifications, which was frowned upon in the theatre, even during rehearsals. He hoped it was the incriminating video that he had demanded. Petri's mind went blank, and he struggled to remember the following lines and blocking. Professor Hakala noticed.

"Petri," she warned softly, "Focus."

The other actors exchanged glances, noticing Petri's distraction, but kept their professionalism. Petri redirected his attention to the play, focusing on his scene with the Firefox. The fox costume was made of black shiny fur that contrasted and highlighted the bright yellow eyes. The flowing tail was equipped with battery-operated fiber-optics; it stayed true to the mythology and was in theme with the season's light festival.

Petri recited, "You may be cunning and clever enough to outsmart a bear. But I am the Menninkäinen. Cross me if you dare!"

Petri viewed the Firefox character as a direct representation of Mikko, defying his threats and trying to outwit him. Petri's intensity in the scene was attention-grabbing, and his emotions got the better of him. The underlying anger and desperation seeped into his performance.

"Tulikettu!" Petri shouted, his voice cracking with emotion. He lunged at the other actor, grabbing him by the collar.

"You think you're so clever, don't you?"

The actor playing the Fox stumbled back, caught off guard by Petri's sudden outburst. His eyes widened in shock as Petri grasped his collar; the intensity of Petri's voice and actions left him momentarily paralyzed with surprise.

"Petri..." he stammered, his own character momentarily forgotten.

Petri immediately apologized, his face flushing with embarrassment.

"Can we take a break? I just need a minute," He requested, his hands still shaking with adrenaline and unresolved frustration. Professor Hakala nodded.

"Sure, let's take a break," she announced.

Petri ran into the wings to check his phone. It wasn't a video, but Mikko had sent a message.

In all caps, it said:

FUCK YOU

T.LI

MUDANGELPUBLISHING.COM

MUDANGELPUBLISHING@GMAIL.COM

 PATREON

PATREON.COM/THESATYRICON

TIKTOK.COM/@LIXINGCHEN1999

@PINKMAGICMOONANDSTARDUST6855

www.ingramcontent.com/pod-product-compliance
Lightning Source LLC
LaVergne TN
LVHW090613110826
845146LV00001B/377

* 9 7 9 8 9 9 1 4 2 2 2 1 5 *